Lock Down Publications and Ca$h
Presents

I0666771

THE
CONNECT'S
SECRET

BUILT FOR A BOSS

Written By
KING RIO

First Edition 2025

Printed in the United States of America

This is a work of fiction. Names, characters, places, and incidents either are products of the author's imagination or are used fictitiously. Any similarity to actual events or locales or persons, living or dead, is entirely coincidental.

Lock Down Publications
P.O. Box 944
Stockbridge, GA 30281
www.lockdownpublications.com

Like our page on Facebook: Lock Down Publications
www.facebook.com/lockdownpublications.ldp

Stay Connected with Us!

Text **LOCKDOWN** to 22828 to stay up-to-date with new releases, sneak peaks, contests and more…

Like our page on Facebook:
Lock Down Publications

Join Lock Down Publications/The New Era Reading Group

Visit our website:
www.lockdownpublications.com

Follow us on Instagram:
Lock Down Publications

Email Us: We want to hear from you!

Chapter 1

Las Vegas
March 2005

Twenty-year-old Tesla Harrison rose from bed, as she did frequently, eager to see her boyfriend, Diego. This afternoon, however, she knew there would be no rolling over into his strong, lean arms, no staring sleepily into his piercing gray eyes.

"When will you be back?" She'd asked when Diego had told her that he and his immediate family were flying to the city of Barranquilla in Colombia, to visit his maternal aunt before she passed away.

"We're staying until after the funeral. Doctors say she only has a couple of days to live, maybe a week. I'd give it ten days tops."

"*Ten days?*"

"It's my aunt, baby. She's dying of pancreatic cancer. I have to be there."

She had sighed miserably. "I understand."

"I'll be back before you know it, crybaby."

"Shut up and get away from me."

He'd slipped his arms around her narrow waist and leaned in for a kiss, and she'd playfully slapped him across the face before succumbing to his tender kisses.

Ten days. Maybe less, maybe more. And, just five days in, Tesla found herself moping around day and night, going through bottles of expensive champagne and binge-watching her favorite movies. *Love Jones. Jason's Lyric. Poetic Justice. A Bronx Tale*. Films that made her miss Diego even more.

Before leaving for Barranquilla, he'd put her up at the Bellagio hotel and Casino, in the lavish $25,000-a-night Blue Sky Villa, a two-story, 8,200-square-foot suite with an elevator and a glass-wall Jacuzzi that overlooked the Las Vegas strip. It was the same suite he'd brought her to after their first date last summer. Since then, she had rarely returned to the blighted neighborhood she'd grown up in on the Westside of Atlanta, and when she did, it was only to bring money and other necessities to her mother and three-year-old daughter, Ferrari.

In the jacuzzi, two of Tesla's closest friends were engaged in a boisterous conversation that was centered around the Black Mafia family, a crew of drug dealers that had recently taken over the streets of Atlanta. The two friends were Rhonda, Tesla's childhood friend from Bowen Homes, and Juicy, the exotic dancer who'd introduced Tesla to the stripper pole three years ago. Juicy and Rhonda had flown in from Atlanta the previous evening. Rhonda had detected a note of melancholy in Tesla's voice during a phone conversation yesterday morning, so she'd called up Juicy and they'd come to Las Vegas on a mission to comfort their girl.

Tesla pieced together an ensemble that consisted of a curve-hugging designer dress, a diamond Tiffany bracelet, and a pair of high-heeled Louis Vuitton pumps. She trapped into the spa-like bathroom, showered, and then stood before the vanity mirror brushing her long waterfall of silky black hair. She had inherited her hair texture, as well as her long eyelashes, jade green eyes, her dimpled cheeks, her high cheekbones, her notably plump lips, and her enormous, round buttocks – from her Cuban mother, Claudia Chavez-Harrison. Growing up in Atlanta's nefarious zone 1 section, Tesla's honey brown complexion and stunningly attractive features had made her the center of attention and perpetual topic of every discussion that pertained to the prettiest girls in the neighborhood. Then, at around the age of fourteen, her hips had spread, and her ass and thighs had swelled and suddenly she'd become the most sought-after girl in Bowen Homes. At sixteen, she'd gotten pregnant by Lorenzo Hollis, a then nineteen-year-old who'd been one of the biggest drug-dealers in Bankhead until he was arrested and sentenced to years in prison for a cocaine possession charge. At seventeen, Tesla dropped out of high school, got her GED, and, using a fake ID, started stripping to support her daughter. By the time she turned eighteen, she'd been cast in more than a dozen hip hop music videos with some of the industry's most preeminent recording artists. She'd been featured on the cover of King magazine twice, and people were still losing their minds over her performance in an unknown Miami rapper's BET Uncut music video, in which she'd made her thick buttocks clap and bounce while she stood on the roof of a sleek black Mercedes G-Wagon.

She put on her pumps. They were yellow, like the Valentino dress, like the pave diamonds in her tennis bracelet. There were also yellow diamonds in the Cartier wristwatch Diego had recently given her. She couldn't remember where she'd left it, but she knew it was here somewhere. She would find it eventually, in one designer bag or another.

She finished up in the bathroom and went out to get her mobile phone off the bedside table. The cellular phone was a black and yellow "Bumblebee" Nextel, and it lay fully charged next to a shaded lamp. Tesla flipped it open, saw that there were no missed calls or new text messages from Diego, and let out a miserable groan.

"Stupid fucking Colombian," she grumbled.

After sending a text to her makeup artist, Tesla picked up the hotel phone and called up room service. She ordered a high-calorie brunch: cheese eggs, dry-aged bone-in rib-eye steak with a side of oxtail marmalade, broiled applewood-cured bacon, orange juice, and whole milk. Then she hung up and got dressed.

A few minutes later, her glam squad arrived. Two hair stylists and one makeup artist, all graduates of the prestigious Paul Mitchell cosmetology school, were staying in a less expensive suite. Big Rick, Tesla's enormous black bodyguard, let them in. Rhonda and Juicy stood talking a few feet away as Tesla sat down in a leather swivel chair and let her glam team get to work.

"Girl, this suite is the business," Rhonda said, her intelligent brown eyes wandering left and right, up and down. Clad in a two-piece bikini and stylish high-heeled sandals, she was a petite, dark-skinned girl with the kind of perfect smile that belonged in a toothpaste commercial and legs that seemed to go on forever. Her dreadlocks were whirled up into a ropy topknot. Her skin was still damp from the jacuzzi. "This place is like a mansion in the sky. I wonder how much they charge per night."

"An arm and a leg and a whole damn eye," Juicy said. "Diego just got it like that. Spend it like it ain't nothing. I hope I can get a rich nigga to walk in the strip club and save me the way Diego saved this heifer. That's the whole reason I started stripping in the first place."

Rhonda was eyeing the crown moldings and the sparkling crystal chandeliers. "I need to start twerking my ass for a sugar daddy. Those school loans are so expensive. I owe something like thirty-eight grand."

"Stripping and twerking actually requires you to have an ass to begin with, and that's something you ain't got. Sorry to break it to you."

Rhonda clucked her tongue and gave Juicy a tight stare. "First off, y'all can stop talking down on my lil booty. Just because you and Tess look like y'all got butt-pregnant from too much butt sex does not give y'all the right to get on mine . I got a nice lil humpback there." She paused and waited for

Juicy and Tesla to stop tittering over the butt-pregnant comment and then sailed on. "And besides, we all know that stripping is not for me. I'm a good girl, and I make more than enough as a photographer. Stripping puts you in contact with too many bad people. Heck, if I wanted to be around gangstas and drug dealers every night, I would've stayed in Bankhead."

It was true. Rhonda made a pretty decent living as a celebrity photographer. Her career had taken off two years ago when she became Tesla's personal photographer. Since then, she'd become the go-to girl for celebrity photo shoots in and around the Atlanta area. She now had a photography studio just around the way from her three-bedroom home in Cascade Heights.

"Speaking of Bankhead," Juicy said, turning to Tesla, "When are you planning on moving Miss Claudia out of Bowen Homes? Whatever happened to that nice house on Church Street she wanted? I thought you had already bought it."

"I did. It's been under renovation since December," Tesla said drably.

Juicy wrinkled her nose at Tesla. "Bitch, if you don't lighten the fuck up. Get outta this funky-ass mood, Tesla. All funkdafied and shit – bitch, you ain't Da Brat. We are in Las motherfucking Vegas, in the most expensive suite these honkeys got, and you in here pouting over a man you met two or three months ago."

"Six and a half months ago," Tesla corrected.

"I wouldn't give a damn if it was six and a half years ago. We are from zone 1, bitch, and zone 1 bitches don't get dick whipped. We do the whipping. Now cheer the fuck up before I kick you in your goddam forehead."

The corners of Tesla's mouth rose into a subtle smirk. She starred Juicy, whose real name was Constance Smith. Juicy's yellowish brown complexion was the direct result of her having interracial parents, a white mother and a black father, the latter of whom had cast her off on his sister so he could smoke his crack in peace after the former was convicted of manslaughter. Juicy was mulatto, or, as mulattos were commonly referred to in the black community, a "Yellowbone," and she was nearly as thick in the thighs and derriere as Tesla. She had Gucci sunglasses and a white one-piece bathing suit with THICK THIGHS SAVE LIVES written across the chest in bold black letters. Gold rings glistened on her perfectly manicured fingers Her hair, colored blond and parted up the middle, was long and straight like Tesla's.

She smiled at Tesla's dim smirk. "There we go. There we fucking go. That's the bitch I introduced to the pole. Make me proud, ho."

Tesla's closed-mouthed smirk widened into an aluminous smile. Shaking her head and choking back a laugh, she raised a middle finger to Juicy and said, "Shut up and get away from me."

Rhonda and Juicy got engaged in a bit of lighthearted name-calling while Tesla ate brunch. All of it was at Tesla's expense. They called her several different kinds of fat bitches. The fact that her waistline, just twenty-five inches around, was the slimmest in the group mattered very little to them. They took one look at the meal Tesla had ordered and from then on, she was a fat greedy bitch, a fat hungry bitch, a sad fat dick-whipped bitch, and, simplest of all, just a plain old fat bitch.

It was all said to lighten the mood, and it worked like a charm. By the time Tesla finished eating, Juicy had rolled two fat cigarillos of dro, and Rhonda had found the elusive yellow diamond Cartier wristwatch tucked away in the side pocket of a Hermes purse. Tesla returned to the bathroom and brushed her teeth—gently this time, so as not to disturb her expertly applied lipstick—then preceded Juicy and Rhonda into a capacious billiards room that had soft white

Versace rugs over while marble flooring, three suspended televisions, and a full bar at the rear with a dope sound system.

Juicy loaded a bootleg copy of T. I.'s 'Urban Legend' album into the compact disc player and pressed play, lighting a blunt and talking to her boyfriend Keyvon on her cell phone as she did it. Tesla went to the pool table and chalked up a cue stick, while Rhonda readied her high-technology Nikon camera for an impromptu photo shoot.

"So," Rhonda said, carefully lowering the camera strap over her head, "if you don't mind me asking – and believe me, I completely understand if you do – how exactly did Diego and his family get so rich? I mean, do you know how much they're worth?"

"I already told you this," Tesla said with an exasperated sigh. She blew the excess chalk off the tip of her cue stick. "His dad, Alvaro, is a big-time real estate investor who started off in the oil-drilling business down in Corpus Christi, Texas. His mom, Dilma, owns a casino in Atlantic City. Alvaro just recently sold a tobacco farming company and a cement factory in Barranquilla, he's the retired CEO of Santos Oil, and his real estate company, Santos Prime Properties, has about two thousand luxury home for sale in the United States and luxury condominiums in Miami, Chicago, New York City, Houston, and Los Angeles. I believe Alvaro also has a lot of stocks and bonds. I don't know all of it. Diego tells me a lot, but I don't remember all of it. I think his dad's net worth is something like nine billion dollars, most of it from stock shares in that oil company. Diego's worth somewhere around four hundred and twenty million."

Rhonda shook her head. "Try seven hundred and forty million. And Alvaro is worth nineteen billion. I looked it up on the internet. Forbes has Diego listed as the wealthiest American bachelor under twenty-five."

Tesla shrugged her shoulders dismissively. "I love Diego for who he is, not for how much money he got. Don't get me wrong, it's definitely a plus. I ain't fucking no broke nigga, but money ain't everything?"

"Did he tell you about the time he and his sister Sofia were kidnapped from a shopping center in Mexico City back in ninety-three?"

"Of course he did. What the fuck is this, an interrogation?"

"I'm just saying. They were kidnapped by a Mexican drug cartel. Alvaro reportedly paid twenty-five million dollars in cash to get them back. The alleged kidnappers, five guys who worked for the Arellano Felix brothers' Tijuana Cartel, were found chopped to pieces in front of Ramon Arellano Felix's compound two weeks after the ransom was paid and Sofia and Diego were released independent investigation later determined that Alvero Santos had likely hired a crew of sicarios from a rival Mexican drug cartel to track down and murder the kidnappers. It was also determined that the cash used to pay the ransom had come directly from Pablo Escobar, the boss of the Medellin drug cartel in Colombia."

Juicy, who'd flipped her phone shut and sidled over to the pool table to pass Tesla the blunt, seemed to have been eavesdropping on the entire conversation. She was unusually attentive, hanging onto Rhonda's every word.

Already baffled by a few details in the story, details that Diego had neglected to tell her, Tesla puffed on the blunt and listened with rapt attention.

"The detectives investigating Alvaro's involvement in the whole mess were told to stand down when they began looking into his connections to the Medellin Cartel, both by their own superiors and the law enforcement officials in Medellin. Long story short, the three detectives decided to expose Alvaro to the American news media to get the story out. They set up a meeting with an investigative journalist from The New York Times. The meeting was supposed to take place on the thirtieth of March, at the very same location where Diego and Sofia were kidnapped. But guess what happened."

"What," Tesla said, feigning disinterest.

"The detectives never made it to that meeting. Never even made it out of their bedrooms. Masked gunmen burst into their homes before dawn and murdered everyone in sight. Carved out the detectives' eyes, sliced off their ears, and cut out their tongues."

"See no evil, hear no evil, speak no evil," Juicy murmured.

"Exactly." Rhonda nodded. "One of the detectives managed to get a shot off before he was killed. He hit one of the gunmen in the head and killed the guy. The dead man turned out to be Alex Garcia, the groomsman from Alvaro's wedding ten years prior. Garcia was also a sicario for the El Padrino drug cartel back in the early eighties."

Rhonda paused for dramatic effect. The pause was totally unnecessary. Tesla and Juicy were all ears. The T.I. song playing in the background – "Motivation," Tesla's favorite song on the album – was suddenly too distant to hear. The blunt burning between Tesla's index and middle fingers hadn't been toked on in nearly sixty seconds.

"And lastly," Rhonda continued, "The New York Times journalist, forty-year-old Kim Raisman –"

"Get the fuck outta hear," Juicy said incredulously.

"Yup. Her too. She was en route to JFK airport to board a Delta flight to Mexico City when it happened. A so-called drunk driver in an eighteen-wheeler practically flattened her tiny little Volvo. He got off easily. A year and eight months on Rikers Island, lost his CDL, mandatory AA meetings, and probation. He swore up and down he'd never heard of the journalist of Alvaro santos when he was questioned by the FBI a year later, but one of Kim Raisman's colleagues, a veteran investigative reporter named Roy Shaffer, later revealed that, back in the eighties, the truck driver had done time for drug trafficking in La Madelo, Colombia's largest prison. His cellmates were none other than Marcos Garcia, the older brother of the groomsman from Alvaro's wedding, and Flix "El Padrino" Gallardo himself. That truck driver – Brian Kelsa is his name – is now living in a four-million-dollar-high-rise apartment in New York City with a young wife and two dogs. He owns a popular sports bar and a construction company, drives a Bentley convertible, and has a maid. FBI can't do anything about it, but Roy Shaffer exposed several bank statements that revealed how his flashy lifestyle is being financed by Alvaro's business associates."

"And where exactly did you learn all this?" Tesla asked, reaching across the pool table to pass Rhonda the blunt. A part of her felt mildly annoyed by Rhonda's intrusion on her and Diego's relationship, but she knew that Rhonda had her best interests at heart.

Rhonda pinched the blunt, brought it up to her lips, and toked. She coughed thrice and then said, "I found it in a New York Times article dated March thirtieth of oh-three, the ten-year anniversary of Kim Raisman's death." She hit the blunt again and coughed so hard that a spittle flew from her mouth and clung to her lower lip. Throwing away the gossamer strands of saliva, she went on. "Look, I'm sorry to be all up in your business like this, I really am, but you're my best friend, and my main concern is your safety. I'd rather see you back with Lorenzo's cheating ass than to see you caught up in some damn drug cartel drama. Diego's fine and all, but he's not worth getting shot or kidnapped over. Go on back to Jazzy T's or Magic City if you have to. Or call up that Packers player who's been hounding you since last year."

Okay, that was it. Tesla rolled her eyes, shook her head, and put an end to the melodrama by splaying her fingertips on the pool table and spearing the chalked end of her tick between her first two fingers, effectively sending the cue ball crashing into the triangle of numbered balls at the opposite end of the table. The nine-ball dropped into the far-left corner pocket, and the game was on. Tesla versus Juicy.

Rhonda's suggestion didn't leave Tesla's mind. It bounced around in there like that translucent green blob from the movie Flubber. The notion of leaving Diego Santos, the man who'd rescued her from the strip club and brought her into his world, a whirlwind of luxury living, limitless spending, and unconditional love – it was too much to consider. She'd need time to think it over. A couple of days, maybe. Then she'd discuss it with Diego and listen to his side of the story. She didn't want to make any rash decisions.

There were good reasons for Tesla's reluctance, the first being that she had recently moved into Diego's 18,000-square-foot Spanish-style mansion in Stone Mountain, Georgia. She'd made the move two months after their first date. He'd purchased the mansion for $22.5 million a week before they met and hadn't gotten around to furnishing it, so he'd given Tesla an American Express black card and a list of world-renowned interior designers and she had taken care of the furnishings. She'd selected a bunch of contemporary artwork, massive screen televisions, state-of-the-art appliances, impossibly comfortable white Italian leather sofas and chairs, and best of all a brand-new high-end designer wardrobe that filled the closets and shelves in her spacious dressing room to full capacity. Diego had also bought her two blacked-out vehicles, a Range Rover and a Ferrari F430. Tesla was living the high life. The idea of leaving it all behind on account of Diego's father's alleged ties to some Colombian drug cartel seemed ludicrous.

And then there was the sex. The raucous, skin-clawing, hair-pulling, hours-long bouts of animalistic sexual pleasure. The thing they did in the bedroom – and in every other room, for that matter – could not even loosely be described as lovemaking it was fucking plain and simple. Pornstar-level fucking. Diego fucked all the strength out of her. He did things to her that her previous sex partners had never done.

14

Sometimes he tied her wrists to the bedposts and ate her pussy for hours on end, often using crushed ice to suck on her clitoris while he fingered her pussy and thumbed her asshole. On Valentine's day, during their four-day vacation at Hotel Twin Dolphin in Los Cabas, Mexico, he'd set up a nice little picnic on the secluded white-sand beach and fucked her for four hours straight. She half-suspected him of taking a Viagra pill that night (he'd shot off five times without ever going flaccid), but she didn't care one way or the other because it had been the best sex she'd ever experienced. There was not a single spot on her body that Diego hadn't orally explored. His main priority was always to get her off first, which usually meant multiple orgasms for her. When he fucked her , only the initial eight or nine strokes were slow and steady. After that there was nothing but savage penetration – rapid, hard-hitting thrusts that made her yelp and moan like a nymphomaniacal madwoman.

Rhonda's camera snapped and whirred.

Juicy's competitive nature compelled her to wager a thousand dollars on the pool game. Never one to be outdone, Tesla upped the ante to twenty-five hundred. She could afford it. Diego had given her four hundred thousand dollars in cash and wired an additional quarter million to her bank account in a thinly veiled attempt to keep her off the pole, and she had already accumulated more than a hundred and ninety grand on her own from stripping, hosting events, and video appearances. She'd brought five ten-thousand-dollar packets of hundred-dollar bills with her from Atlanta, and she had yet to spend any of it.

"Best out of three," Juicy said from behind a haze of dro smoke.

"Best out of three," Tesla agreed. "Then we're hitting the casino and betting it all on the craps table. Rhonda, put down that damn camera and pour up some shots. We got Henny and shot glasses behind the bar."

Four more photos of Tesla were snapped before Rhonda crossed the room to pour the drinks, photos that would likely end up being uploaded to Tesla's website or sold to magazines like XXL, The Source, Hip Hop Weekly, and King. Tesla was a regular in those publications. Her exotic features and fat round derriere were the talk of the industry. Curvaceous women like Buffie the Body and Melyssa Ford were paving the way for bootylicious girls like herself to emerge from the relative obscurity of strip clubs and rap videos to become celebrities in their own right. Maybe not A-listers like Diego's cadaverous sister Sofia, a world famous super-model frequently featured in powerhouse publications like Marie Claire, Vague, Vanity Fair, and People, but Tesla was okay with that. She didn't give a damn what White America thought of her anyway. Her demographic was the black community, and as it stood she was the black community's most popular video vixen and the most talked about stripper in the south. Her fame had only risen since she and Diego started dating six and a half months ago. Now she had the love and life she'd always wanted, and the financial backing she'd always needed. Now she was working with a prolific Italian fashion designer to create *Curtoure*, a clothing line specifically for women with the kind of curves she herself possessed. Now she was the owner of four rental properties on the westside of Atlanta. Now when she and her girls went out for a night on the town, and her haters saw her stepping out of Diego's triple-black Rolls-Royce Phantom or her brand-new Ferrari, they could not help but to become congratulators.

The more Tesla ruminated about the many benefits of dating Diego Santos, the more she realized that, even if his father really was tied to Colombia's infamous Medellin drug cartel, she was willing to stick by his side through thick and thin.

No matter what, Tesla was not leaving Diego Santos.

Chapter 2

No matter what, Diego was not leaving Tesla Harrison.

"She's a fucking stripper, for heaven's sake!" Alvaro bellowed into his son's face. "A ghetto stripper from some shithole project building in Atlanta! And you seriously mean to marry that girl? No! Fuck no! Over my dead body."

Inherently calm and calculated, Diego kept his composure. They were standing poolside near the cabana behind Alvaro's obnoxiously spacious Barranquilla mega mansion, which stood on eighty-five sprawling acres overlooking the pristine blue waters of the Caribbean Sea. Inside the cabana, Diego's mother Dilma lay supine on a chaise longue, barefoot and clad in an expensive shoulder less black dress, her toned brown legs crossed at the ankles. Her distraught gray eyes were concealed behind dark designer sunglasses. A fat fifteen-carat diamond weighed down her ring finger. She was nursing her fourth martini of the afternoon, excluding the one she'd spilled in the limo during their long odyssey home from her sister Anabel's burial.

Alvaro was a lanky man of sixty-three with thin gray hair encircling his balding pate and pale, malefic blue eyes. Like Diego, he wore a black Zegna suit, a dark red shirt and pocket square, and a black silk tie. Both he and Diego were tall, clean and remarkably handsome. They had the same ears, the same cleft chins, the same strong jawlines. They both walked the same confident gait, smiled the same idiosyncratic half-smile. But that was where their similarities ended.

The suit Diego wore had been specially tailored to fit his lithe, athletically-built figure, and it fit him perfectly. Alvaro's, however, was a bit loose around the midsection, as he had developed a slight stoop in recent years. Diego had Dilma's soft gray eyes, curved nose, and unblemished hazel-brown skin; Alvaro was pallid, his eyes perpetually red-veined from decades of alcohol and drug abuse, the lines around his mouth deeply creased from the thousands of cigarettes and cigars he'd smoke over the years. Diego was known for being contemplative, cool-headed, and debonair; Alvaro had a reputation for being ill-tempered and callous. Alvaro had an ego the size of Texas; Diego was not at all egotistical. He was unequivocally the most humble person in the Santos family.

"Love is love, and I love my woman. Can't help who you fall in love with," Diego said, averting his eyes to the thirty or more black-suited guests who'd followed Alvaro's Mercedes limo here from Anabel's burial in a convoy of armored black SUVs. four of them were Aunt Anabel's children, two adult boys and two adult girls, an even split. Anabel's husband, Pao, stood at one end of the Olympic-size pool looking ashen and disheveled, hardly saying a word as Uncle Jesus, Dilma, and Anable's younger brothers, and Uncle Mateo, Alvaro's only sibling, stood conversing on either side of him. Diego wasn't all that familiar with the others, though he'd seen many of them around Alvaro in the past.

"You're too young to be married, Diego. Live a little, when I was your age, I had more women than I have toes and fingers. I must have fucked every beauty queen in Medellin. It's the money, Mijo, that attracts them like flies to shit. I'm telling you, you're going to meet thousands and thousands of women, girls that'll look just as heart-stopping as your cute little stripper. If black girls with jumbo butts is your thing, go to any black strip club in the states and fly the most fat-assed women in there to our family villa in Barcelona for a week. Buy them a hundred feet of that good Indian hair and they'll suck you off until their tonsils fall down their throats. I'm an ass man too, you know, so I understand where you're coming from. Have fun with the girl. Fuck her brains out. But for heaven's sake, don't marry her. Marry a lawyer, a doctor, a fucking shrink. Anybody but a stripper."

"Mom was a bikini model when you married her," Diego pointed out.

"Yeah, and her father was a pediatric neurosurgeon in New York City. know what that means? Your mother won't be hell-bent on getting my money if we ever split. I bet your girl has never even met her father. Marry her and you'll be out of half your fortune in three or four years."

"I'll take your misogynistic opinion into consideration." Diego snatched a furtive glance at his gold Rolex wrist watch. The time was 5:15 pm Eastern, which meant it was a quarter past two in Vegas. Tesla was likely awake. She was a night owl, accustomed to staying up till three or four in the morning and sleeping till around noon. "And really, you've got to stop listening to Sofia. I never said anything about getting married. What I said was 'Tesla would make a great wife,' and Sofa heard exactly that. She twisted my words to make you upset with me. You played right into it."

The lava in Alvaro's hard blue eyes coaled a bit. He switched gears. "We've got a new arrangement with those fuckers in northeast Mexico," he said, and Diego knew without asking that his father was referring to the upper-echelon members of the Matatmoros drug cartel, also known as the Costilla cartel. "They threatened to take their business elsewhere if we didn't lower our prices. I considered waiting a while to see if they'd really try to do it, but that old grinch Vida is about as evil as she is ugly. Like Griselda Blanco on steroids. She'd have burned us in the end. We'll still profit hand over fist, just not as much."

"What are the new prices?"

"Two grand for every pound. Forty-four hundred U.S. dollars per kilo."

"You should've held out."

"And lose our second biggest customer? Are you nuts? I gave her that deal and she immediately ordered thirty tons. Thirty long tons. That's thirty thousand fucking kilos, and she'll probably be making that same order three or four times a year."

"Doesn't sound like that good of a deal to me. We'll get … a hundred and thirty-two million for that thirty-ton deal. She'll sell each kilo to the Americans for sixteen grand a piece, which means, off that thirty tons, she'll make … four hundred and eighty-million dollars. And that's before she cut the product. When it's all said and done she'll make somewhere around six hundred and fifty million. You should've held out. She should be paying the standard five grand per kilo."

"You don't know Vida Costilla. She might have taken my firm stance as a challenge, and that could have easily led to a war. No one challenges that old hag and lives to tell the tale. Besides, we've got eleven other Mexican drug cartels to deal with, not to mention the Puerto Ricans, the Dominicans, and the Jamaicans. We're still clearing a billion and a half annually."

Diego gave a subtle nod, twisting and tugging on the gold ring he wore on the pinkie finger of his left hand as he did it. Rising from the top of the ring were his initials, DS, both letters encrusted with sparkling white VVS diamonds. Intricately carved, teeth-bearing piranhas were engraved into the gold band. Every man on the premises wore an identical pinkie ring with their own diamond encrusted initials.

Over the past five years, Alvaro had invested thousands of hours into teaching his youngest son the ins and outs of the illicit drug market, grooming Diego for the eventual takeover of the second-most powerful cocaine empire in Colombia.

"I have to admit," Alvaro went on, puffing on his Cuban cigar, "I fear Vida Castilla's son more than I do her. He's the epitome of evil."

"Her son?"

"Yeah. Juan Costilla. They call him Papi. deadliest fucker you'll ever meet. You'd do well to steer clear of him." Alvaro had a tall glass of fifty-year-old Macallan whiskey in his other hand. $87,000-a-bottle. He raised the glass to his thin lips and took a small, face-contorting swallow. "Those fuckers in Matamoros are savages. Madmen. Fucking lunatics. No different than the Sinaloa cartel. Cut off your hand to say hello. We were almost as brutal in the Escobar era – managing a cartel takes a cold heart and an iron fist, no way around that – but we never cut off any heads. It's imperative that you keep your cool at all times in this business. Don Pablo was a great man, the greatest of the great, and had he controlled his temper, had he not blown that airliner out of the sky and ended the assassinations of all his political opponents, he'd be standing here with us today?"

Alvaro was always speaking highly of legendary Colombian drug Caesar Pablo Escobar. Once upon a time the two men had been close friends, as evidenced by the ancient photo albums and VHS tapes Alvaro was fond of showing every year around the holidays. There were hundreds of photos and dozens of videos with Pablo in them. Most were taken inside of Alvaro's multimillion-dollar West Palm Beach mansion, the architectural masterpiece of glass, marble and steel where Diego and Sofia were born and raise, but some of the older videos showed Pablo and Alvaro joyriding dirt bikes through the jungles of Medellin with a rowdy group of male friends, and partying at Casa Napoles, Pablo's massive Medellin estate. Diego's memories of Don Pablo were always vague until the photo albums and video tapes came out. Then they became brilliantly clear. Pablo Escobar had been the best godfather a kid could ask for. He'd showered Diego and Sofia with gifts. He'd sat them on his knees and told them the most hilarious stories. He'd paid $500,000 to have Selena Quintanilla perform at Sofia's tenth birthday celebration. The exact details of Alvaro's role in Pablo's drug cartel were unclear to Diego, but he knew that it had ultimately led to Alvaro creating a cartel of his own.

Alvaro's drug cartel was often referred to as either the Barranquilla cartel or the Piranha cartel, but to the ever-growing list of crooked judges, lawyers, bankers, politicians, journalist, and law enforcement officials who routinely accepted cash bribes in exchange for their collusion with the lucrative drug empire, the Barranquilla cartel was nothing more than a myth, a fictional drug cartel conceived by the irrational minds of right-wing conspiracy theorists for the sole purpose of riling up the two million citizens of Barranquilla.

In truth, the Barranquilla cartel was a multilateral drug operation that produced roughly thirty-five to forty percent of the cocaine that made it into Mexico and eventually into the United States every year. Alvaro employed hundreds of farmers and millions of dollars' worth of farming equipment to efficiently till and harvest over five thousand acres of coca fields in northern Colombia and Vraem Valley, Peru. head three subterranean processing plants where the coca was made into cocaine and packaged into kilogram bricks. He used a complex network of airplanes, shipping containers, and military-grade submarines to get the coke into Mexico. A diverse group of high-paid accountants and lawyers managed the money laundering and bribing as they saw fit and filtering the cash through myriad offshore accounts. The Barranquilla cartel was a herculean machine that grossed roughly a hundred million dollars a month and employed thousands. Diego knew the cartel biz inside and out. What he hadn't learned from Alvaro and Uncle Mateo he'd taught himself, through diligent and often tedious research.

He snatched another glance at his wristwatch. "I need to get going." He said, wondering what Tesla was doing, what she was wearing, whether she was missing him or enjoying the alone time.

"You'll get going soon enough," Alvaro said. "First you sit through the introductions. All these busy men have taken the day off not only to pay their respects to your dear Aunt Anabel but also to meet you. Smile your way through the handshakes and then you can return to your pretty little stripper."

Despite the obviously negative connotation, Diego's heart swelled at the idea of returning to his 'pretty little stripper'. He knew exactly what introductions were about to take place. He'd been waiting years for this moment. Although he knew the names and positions of every man in the Barranquilla cartel hierarchy, he'd never been formally introduced to most of them. He couldn't match the names with the face; the introductions would do that for him.

Now he understood why, shortly before Aunt Anabel's funeral, he'd finally received his piranha ring.

The introduction was the final in Diego's ascension to the very top of the cartel. He would be the underboss until Alvaro either retired or passed away.

Then Diego would become the reigning boss of the Barranquilla cartel.

An hour and twenty minutes later, Diego and Sofia arrived at Barranquilla Airport private terminal area in a black Cadillac limousine. They found the tarmac before the hangars occupied by two dozen private planes, most of them single - and twin - engine propeller models. Except one: a Gulfstream G650 jet. At sixty-five-million dollars, the G6 was not only the world's most expensive executive jet but also the fastest, capable of almost a Mack 1 top speed, with a range of more than eight thousand miles and a ceiling of fifty thousand feet.

The G6 belonged to Diego, or "Colombiano", as he was known to friends and family alike, was currently ranked 421st on Forbes's richest people list, with a net worth of seven hundred and forty million dollars and he was fiercely determined to make it to the top 100.

Having started out in 2000 as a sixteen-year-old intern at Santos Prime Properties, Diego had by the age of eighteen sold more than a hundred luxury properties, half of which he'd purchased and flipped himself using the $100 million had given him. This along with his astonishing understanding of the stock market (he'd been an avid reader of The Wall Street Journal since the age of twelve) had set him on a path to perpetual prosperity. By twenty, he had quintupled his net worth to $500 million; by twenty-two, he would undoubtedly be worth more than a billion.

That being said, Diego was in his daily life conspicuous and impeccably dressed, often cruising around the city of Atlanta in his matte-black 2005 Rolls-Royce Phantom and dining at exclusive Michelin starred restaurants. Somewhat of a recuse and a stickler for privacy, he was seldom photographed in public, and when he did attend events, whether business or social, he usually did so virtually via webcam.

Sofia looked at Diego. "I'm sorry to break it to you," she said, "but I went through the introductions eight months ago. You're not all that important."

"Your introductions were merely a formality. You know that. Also, over the years, I've grown impervious to your simple-minded insults. I thought you'd have caught on to that by now," Diego replied.

"Yeah, well, I thought you'd have wisened up by now. That girl only wants you for your money. You're going to marry a gold digger."

"Why are you so concerned with my personal life?"

"I'm concerned because you're my brother and you've fallen for a stripper. All she wants to do is lure you in – which she's done quite successfully, by the way – get you to marry her, get you to impregnate her, and then she'll take half your net worth in the divorce and live off your hard-earned dollars for the rest of her life. She'll live off child support and alimony after you in the same way she probably lived off government assistance before you."

"Your ignorance has no bounds."

"You're the ignorant one."

Diego regarded his sister with an indecipherable stare. He wanted to choke her. Seated at the opposite end of the long leather seat, Sofia was clad in a red silk blouse and a black knee-length pencil skirt. Her long bronze legs were crossed, and she had a pair of open-toed Gucci heels strapped to her flawlessly pedicured feet. These days all she wore was Gucci; she had a five-year, ten-million dollar modeling contract with the high-end fashion line. She stood nearly six feet tall. Last year she'd been named the worlds' most beautiful woman by People magazine. Her current beau was Emili Rivera, star pitcher of the Los Angeles Dodgers. They lived together in a twenty-million-dollar west Hollywood mansion.

Sofia's impossibly pretty visage was fixed in a malevolent sneer, and there was ice in her steel blue eyes. Her hair was done in a neat golden blond long bob. Her red-pointed lips matched her expertly manicured fingernails. A piranha ring with her initials glistened on the pinkie finger of her left hand. She was the only girl to own one.

Ignoring his sister's inflammatory remarks, Diego looked out his window as his two bodyguards and her two bodyguards emerged from two Escalades and removed their luggage from the rear storage compartments. Diego shoved open his door before the chauffeur could open it for him. He stepped out of the limo and thumbed open his Nextel flip-phone. Sofia climbed out next. Diego's intention had been to phone Tesla, but now he changed his mind. He was too agitated to be making phone calls. His expression didn't show it, but Sofia had gotten under his skin.

They showed their passports to a guard, then followed the guard through a pedestrian gate to the gulf stream's lowered stairs. Pari Moussari, Diego's personal chef and sometime flight attendant, a short middle-aged Middle Eastern woman with caterpillar eyebrows and a gap-toothed smile, stood waving at the top of the red-carpeted steps. Once aboard, they found themselves in the small but neatly appointed galley where Pari was known to prepare some of the finest dishes known to man. To the right, through an archway, was the main cabin. The bulkheads were covered in gleaming walnut inlaid with gold fist-sized piranha emblems, the floor in plush black Versace carpet. There were two seating areas, one a group of four tan leather recliner seats around a coffee table, the second, aft, a trio of overstuffed settees. Beyond that, through a second archway, was a bedroom that boasted thick Versace rugs and Versace linen on a king-size bed. The air was cool and air-conditioned. Softly, through unseen speakers, came Jay-Z's "99 Problems".

"Drop me off at LAX first," Sofia grumbled snappishly.

A deep baritone with a heavy Spanish accent said, "I'm no psychic, but something tells me you two rich brats have been arguing again. Am I right?"

From one of the rearward-facing recliner seats a man rose and faced them. He was six foot four, two hundred twenty pounds – nearly all of it was muscle – with a tan face and short, carefully styled raven hair. His name was Lazaro Santos, and he was Uncle Mateo's 27-year-old son. He smiled broadly at them; his teeth were square and perfectly white.

Arms outstretched, he strode towards them. He wore the black three-piece Zegna suit he'd worn to the funeral, a piranha ring, a gold Rolex, and snake-skin cowboy boots. Diego and Sofia looked down at the boots.

Lazaro didn't miss their expressions. "Don't give me that look Snake's I this season, you two just haven't caught up." He hugged Sofia first, then Diego. "I already spoke with the pilot. LAX it is Sofe. Then Diego and I are Vegas-bound, baby! And you know what they say: what happens in Vegas, stays in Vegas."

"We've got a lot of networking to do," Diego said.

"No. No networking. No working at all. Vegas is not the place you go when there's work to do. I lost three hundred and fifty thousand last time I was there, and I intend to get all that back this go around. Come on and get seated. Get the drinks flowing."

"You know this nerd only wants water," Sofia said, and hooked a thumb at Diego. "I'll take a vodka straight."

"Pari, if you don't mind," Lazaro said. "I'll have the same."

"Fiji," Diego said tersely.

From close behind Diego and Sofia, Pari said, "Yes, Mr. Santos."

They followed Lazaro to the recliner area and sat down. Pari was only seconds behind them with a tray. She placed Sofia's and Lazaro's drinks before them and handed a bottle of Fiji water to Diego. He accepted the bottle, scowled across the coffee table at Sofia, and shook his head. Through strongly clenched teeth he said, "One of these days your big mouth is going to get you in a heap of trouble … with me."

"Ooouuu. I'm petrified. Look, Lazaro – it's Geekzilla."

Lazaro said nothing. He knew better than to speak for either party in Diego and Tesla's turbulent sibling rivalry.

Leaning forward in his seat, glaring daggers at his sister, Diego said, "Emilio's southpaw, isn't he?"

Sofia looked confused. "Southpaw?"

"Yeah. Southpaw. Left-handed." Diego stared at her, a sinister smirk burgeoning on his face, until she narrowed her eyelids and sneered. "Tell me," he urged. "Is he left-handed? I'm really curious to know."

"Don't you fucking dare," Sofia muttered.

"It'd be a shame if some idiot with a machete hacked off Emilio's fingers in a failed robbery attempt. Especially if it happened to be the fingers of his left hand. He'd never play again." He twisted the top of his bottle of Fiji water and took a drink. The expressions flashing across Sofia's flawless features – a complex mixture of trepidation, uncertainty, and unbridled fury – brought an even broader smirk to Diego's face. "I'm done playing these games with you, Sofia. One way or another, you're gonna respect me."

"I never disrespected you."

"Yeah, you did. You do it all the time. But you crossed the line when you disrespected my woman. I'm giving you forty-eight hours to apologize. After that it's off with his hand." Diego turned to Lazaro. The G6 was taxiing toward the runway. "We need to establish a distribution network within the United States. It's past time we cut out the Mexicans. They're making billions every month. That money should be ours. If my father won't do anything about it, I will."

Lazaro nodded. "I know people. We can make it happen."

Arms folded across her chest, Sofia glowered at Diego. She was seething with anger. A single tear trickled down from her left eye. The toe of one high-heeled shoe drummed incessantly at the side of the coffee table. Her nostrils flared and her jaw muscles flexed. Her breaths were deep and shaky.

Diego reclined his chair and smiled pleasantly. He took a long drink of water, sighed contentedly, and said, "There's a new Sheriff in town, Sofe. I'd advise you to get on the right side of the law."

Chapter 3

Tesla was on a roll.

She'd beaten Juicy on the pool table, and now, ten floors below her luxurious hotel site, she was up twenty-seven thousand dollars on the craps table. Rhonda and Juicy stood on either side of her, cheering her on. A group of excited hangers-on had gathered around them; Big Rick, who was six foot seven and over two hundred fifty pounds, kept them at a comfortable distance. He was a mid-thirties man with a bald head and cool-black skin. His formidable size was enough to keep the growing crowd at bay.

Four rolls later Tesla crapped out and lost three grand. "Whelp, I'm done," she said, and there was a collective sigh from the hangers-on as she collected her hundred-dollar chips from the table.

"Let's hit the slot machines," Rhonda suggested.

"I gotta pee first," Tesla said.

The four of them – Tesla, Rhonda, Juicy and Big Rick – headed for the restrooms, which happened to be just beyond the slot machines. Halfway there, Tesla's cell phone rang in her purse. She dug it out of her croc-skin Hermes Birkin bag and looked to see who was calling, hoping it was Diego.

It was not.

"Who is that?" Asked the ever-inquisitive Rhonda Evergreen. She had on a white designer jumpsuit and matching heels, and she was nursing a strawberry daiquiri through a straw.

"Nobody but Enzo's annoying ass," Tesla said.

Enzo was short for Lorenzo. He had first taken on the nickname as an aspiring rap artist five years prior. He'd stopped rapping to focus on trapping shortly thereafter, but the name had stuck. He'd only been out of prison a month and half and already he was back to selling crack, this time out of a seedy motel on the east side of Atlanta. He and Keyvon, Juicy's boyfriend, hustled together at a Knights Inn on Bouldercrest Road. Tesla hated that Enzo was dealing crack again, but she understood why he was doing it. His and Tesla's daughter, Ferrari, was well taken care of, but he had two more daughters by the two girls he'd cheated on Tesla with before he went to prison.

She answered the call and told him to hold on until she got in the restroom.

Enzo had never been a particularly good listener. "Where you at?" He asked, but she ignored him and kept walking toward the restroom.

She and Juicy were the recipients of numerous gawking stares as they sashayed through the casino. Their ample curves were accentuated by their tight-fitting dresses. Juicy measured forty-three inches around the hips, Tesla a staggering forty-eight. They were used to being gaped at when they wore tight clothes.

In the restroom, Tesla made Enzo wait a moment longer. She squatted in the first unoccupied stall and emptied her bladder, then swiped her vagina with a wet wipe and raised the Nextel to her ear.

"Boy, what the hell do you want?"

"Where you at?"

"I'm in Vegas. Why?"

He hesitated. "The fuck you doin' in Vegas?"

"I'm doing what I 'm supposed to be doing. Minding my own business. You should try it sometime." She used the bottom of her shoe to flush the toilet. "What do you want, Lorenzo?"

"I wanna see my baby. Her sister got a birthday party this Wednesday. I want all my kids to be there."

"Okay. she'll be there. Is that all?"

"Nah. I need some money too."

Tesla sucked her teeth indignantly. "I shoulda known."

"Damn, don't kick me when I'm down. You know I hate askin' people for shit. I wouldn't be askin' if I didn't need it. It ain't like I can just go out and find a job. These crackers ain't hiring no convicted felons. Shit, I got three kids to take care of, probation fees, rent, insurance, and I just had to get some new brake pads and tires put on my Chevelle."

"Okay," Tesla said, rolling her eyes, "First off, you can eliminate my baby from that list of kids you gotta take care of, because Rari is well taken care of. The only thing she needs from you is quality time. Secondly, you just put those big-ass chrome rims on that car, got a new paint job, new interior. That shit ain't cheap. You should've paid probation with the money you blew on that damn car."

"Kick me when I'm down," Enzo repeated glumly.

"I should have 'Kicked' you in your damn nuts for having two babies behind my back. But no, what did I do? I 'Kicked' your lawyer eight thousand dollars and got your prison sentence modified from twenty years to three years. Then I 'Kicked' you another ten thousand dollars when you got out of prison and found out your so-called girlfriend had sold all your shit. So you can miss me with all this crybaby bullshit. I ain't got time for it. Tell me how much you need and I'll see what I can do."

A longer hesitation. "I need like twenty -five thousand," he said finally.

Tesla scoffed at the amount. "I'll give you twenty-five thousand dollars when you suck on this pussy for twenty-five thousand hours." Stepping out of the stall, she heard Juicy and Rhonda burst out laughing and saw the wide-eyed looks on the faces of two drunk-lookin' Hispanic girls.

"You got jokes," Enzo said, but he couldn't help chuckling himself. "At least let me get twelve-five so I can fuck my five-oh-four girl?"

He was speaking in code. Five-oh-four girls meant five hundred and four grams of coke, half of a kilo, the going price for which was roughly twelve grand. Knowing Enzo, he would probably mix the cocaine with baking soda and cook it into about six hundred and ten grams of crack. He'd sell small rocks of it to the junkies and make about $1,700 off every ounce. Tesla had watched him do it too many times to count, and then she'd begun cooking it for him. Once she had cooked two whole 36-ounces kilos into eighty-eight ounces of crack. That had been for her brother Marlon, another big-time dope boy out of Bowen Homes. Marlan was currently in Fulton County jail serving a nine-month sentence for probation violation. He was due home next month.

"I'll see what I can do," Tesla said.

"Don't act like you ain't got it. Everybody in the hood knows you got it. You done got famous off the lil magazine and video features, and now you got some rich Mexican takin' care of you. Gotchoo all iced out, pushin' Ferrari's and Range Rovers, dressin' all fancy and shit. Don't forget about the nigga who was there for you before the rap videos and magazine covers. I shouldn't have to beg you for no money."

Tesla opened her mouth to say yeah, well, you shouldn't have cheated on me, but Enzo hung up before she could get a single word of it out. She folded the cell phone shut and squeezed it as if she meant to break it. "I fucking hate him," she said, really meaning it.

They ate a light dinner at White Falcon, a 5-star restaurant on another floor of the towering Bellagio. Tesla phoned her mom, who was in the middle of a ridiculous argument with Tesla's three-year-old daughter. Claudia didn't want a god in her house because she thought they smelled like we white people; Ferrari opined that dogs were pretty and they were good at biting bag guys. The innocuous dispute brought a warm smile to Tesla's face, effectively ridding her of the lingering contempt she'd felt from her phone call with Enzo.

After dinner they left the Bellagio and hit an all-male strip club. Somehow Rhonda managed to get pulled on stage for a personal dance from a muscled-up Jamaican stud in a black thong. Juicy picked up Rhonda's digital camera and snapped away, laughing and cheering with Tesla as she did it.

"That's about as close as she done got to some dick since she moved out of Zone 1," Juicy said, and slapped her knee with laughter.

Tesla couldn't take her eyes off the spectacle. The Jamaican was a gift from God. his arms and his shoulders and his bulging pectoral muscles, all oiled and glistering in the glaring flashes from Rhonda's camera. His perfectly outlined six-pack and the long fat snake outlined in his thong underwear. It all made for an irresistible show. Tesla wanted a piece of that well-endowed Jamaican man; she regretted the temptation, what with her being as crazy in love with Diego and all, but the temptation was definitely there.

An hour later, the three of them stalked out of the strip club ahead of Big Rick and piled into their chauffeured party bus, a sparkly-interior boxy thing with two stripper poles, a minibar, and several televisions spread throughout it. Juicy flirted shamelessly with Big Rick as they cruised Las Vegas Boulevard, impervious to the wedding ring on his ring finger and the pregnant wife she knew was waiting for him back home in Atlanta. Tesla and Rhonda watched with stunned expressions as Juicy gave him a provocative lap dance, grinding and twerking her meaty buttocks on his crotch. When she finally climbed off of him, Tesla observed with a growling smile that the front of his pants was sticking out. And when Juicy went to her knees between his legs and began undoing his pants, Tesla observed with widening eyes that Big Rick had a big penis. Incredibly big. Juicy had to tug and wrestle it out of his underwear, and when she finally got it out Rhonda let out a gasp and grabbed Tesla's wrist.

Big Rick's dick was at least ten inches in length, and its girth was so thick that Tesla didn't think she could take it vaginally, let alone orally. Juicy, however, had no problem wrapping her big mouth around it.

"Oh my God," Rhonda said.

"Fucking freaks," Tesla said

But she was not disgusted or even mildly put off by the overt sexual act. Neither was Rhonda. The two of them watched in stunned silence as Juicy spit and slurped on Big Rick's sizable appendage. Tesla found herself becoming wet from the mere sight of the intense blowjob. Big Rick sat back in his seat, wearing an open-mouthed grin that was an eye-catching display of porcelain-white teeth in a pitch-black face. "Ooouuu, shit, you da truth," he avowed, eliciting a burst of titters from Rhonda and an explosive guffaw from Tesla.

Juicy used a lot of spit. It was her notoriously sloppy blow jobs that had gotten her the nickname Juicy nearly a decade ago, when she had sucked off two high school basketball players in a Bowen Homes stairwell. Tesla and Rhonda had watched her then just as they were watching her now, and by the looks of it Juicy had only gotten better with time.

Big Rick barely lasted five minutes before he spewed a creamy mouthful of cum into Juicy's steadily sucking mouth. Tesla got up and stood beside Juicy to get a good look at the messy aftermath. There was a lot of semen in Juicy's big mouth. Viscous white strands of it dangled from the roof of her mouth to her tongue, from her upper teeth to the bottom ones. It looks as if she'd sucked all the contents out of a bottle of Elmer's school glue. She smacked the fat hand of Big Rick's dick on her tongue, then closed her mouth and swallowed.

They arrived at the Bellagio minutes later and crossed paths with a group of handsome young black men in town from Boston for a bachelor party. The guys were conversing boisterously near the elevators. Their eyes lit up when they saw Tesla. They recognized her from a recently released 50 cents music video. She stopped briefly to say hi, showing a grateful smile as she did it, then she and her crew went to the elevator. The reflective steel doors were parting when Juicy turned to the bachelor boys and said, "We're about to put on some bathing suits and head out to the swimming pool ... in case y'all tryna kick it, you know."

"We'll be there," one of the boys said quickly.

"With balls on," said another.

Tesla rolled her eyes and shook her head, but she didn't say anything, not even in her head. She had taken one too many shots of cognac and was all smiles. The weed she'd smoked probably had something to do with it too. Mostly, though, it was the company of her two best friends that had her in such a good mood. Juicy may have been a disloyal girlfriend to Keyvon, but she was a damned good friend to Tesla and Rhonda.

The elevator doors slid closed, and Tesla said, "I don't know why you just lied to them like that. I'm about to kick these heels off, order some popcorn, and watch *Love Jones* for the fifty-leventh time."

"I'm with you, Tess," Rhonda said. "I'm way too tipsy to be hanging out with people I don't know. You see what happened to those four construction workers. Somebody probably caught them high and drunk."

Tesla gave Rhonda a look. "They found them?" She had seen the faces of the four missing men on a billboard near Lenox Square Mall just last week. There was another billboard with their pictures on it on the side of Interstate 20. The men had gone missing two months ago. Their disappearances had been all over the news stations lately. One of the men had worked part-time as a bouncer at

Strokers, a strip club Tesla had danced at a couple times in the past. Everybody called him Ron Ron, and though Tesla couldn't remember ever meeting him, she'd heard nothing but good things about him.

"Mm hmm. They found 'em, a'ight – what was left of 'em," Juicy said, folding a stick of chewing gum onto her tongue. "I figured you had heard."

"Yeah," Rhonda said. "Some lady found five dead bodies in a field somewhere out by those abandoned buildings on Greenbriar Parkway. The coyotes ate them up pretty good, but they died from gunshot wounds."

Tesla furrowed her brow. "*Five* bodies?"

Rhonda nodded. "The fifth man, whoever he is, was never reported missing. The bodies were found two days ago. I'm surprised you didn't see it on the news."

Tesla hadn't watched a news channel since her first day in the suite. She shook her head at the startling revelation, but she wasn't all that surprised. Homicides were a common occurrence in Atlanta. The vast majority of them were gang-related or drug-related. She figured the four dead men and their friend had likely ripped off the wrong drug-dealer and paid for it with their lives.

Still, she wondered what kind of man could be so heartless as to murder five men in cold blood. She was suddenly reminded of how incredibly fortunate she was to have a good man like Diego on her side. He had taken her out of the perilous and often self-destructive Atlanta nightlife and into the safety of his world, a tantalizing vision of private jets and oversize mansions.

A magnetized keycard was needed to unlock the heavy wooden sliding doors of Tesla's sky-high suite. She used it, Big Rick parted the doors … and there stood Diego Santos.

Chapter 4

Tesla's eyes, which had been at half-mast, flew open wide. She gasped, leapt into Diego's arms, and wrapped her legs around his waist. The subtle smell of his cologne whelmed her senses.

"Baby!" She screamed. She held his gorgeous face in her hands and kissed his soft, smiling lips repeatedly. The others laughed, but she didn't care. She hardly even noticed them. Right now it was just her and Diego; no one else mattered.

"I take it … you missed me," he said in between kisses.

"*Missed you*? Boy, if you *ever* leave me alone like that again, you and I are going to have some serious problems." Tears of joy had welled up in her eyes, and now she blinked them away. Diego gave her a sharp two-handed swat on the ass. She inhaled shakily through flared nostrils and nibbled at her lower lip.

From somewhere behind Tesla, Rhonda said, "Okay, Juicy, I'm with you. We're going swimming with the Boston boys." Tesla dropped her feet to the travertine marble floor, grabbed a hold of Diego's necktie, and pulled him toward the staircase that led up to the master bedroom suite. The alcohol coursing through her veins had her libido on a whole other level. She wanted to feel his body on top of hers, and beneath hers, and behind hers. Her clitoris craved the attention of his agile tongue, and she wanted to taste the warm, silky hardness of his dick in her mouth; she was no cum-gulping fellatio expert like Juicy, but she knew how to properly and effectively suck a dick.

The spiral staircase in the Blue Sky Villa's marble floored foyer was beautiful. It rose from the center of the first floor and expanded outward as it wound to the second floor. The staircase ended just outside the master bedroom suite, where it was capped by a gold and crystal chandelier that brightened the stairs all the way down.

Diego put his hands on Tesla's hips as they climbed the stairs. He kissed the rear of her right shoulder. An intense heat blossomed deep down in her belly, and her excited smile grew wider. She shouted down to Big Rick, told him to accompany Rhonda and Juicy out to the swimming pool. He nodded his shiny black, bald head and disappeared into a bathroom, while Juicy and Rhonda scurried off to put on their swimsuits.

"I bought you something," Diego said, peppering the crock of her neck with several more light smooches.

"I just want some dead. Give me that and I'll be A-okay."

"Dead?"

"Yes, some dick and some head. Give me both and I'll be in heaven."

Diego laughed heartily. "Good one. Good one. First time I've heard that one."

"I came up with that about a year ago. Had all the Bankhead bitches sayin' it."

"Well, I've got some dead for you, and I brought you a few gifts too."

"Win-win," Tesla said as they reached the top of the staircase.

She let go of his tie and entered the bedroom ahead of him. To her surprise, she found a neatly compartmentalized black carrying case lying open on the bed. Wedged into one of the velvety compartments was a sparkling gold handgun. As Tesla moved closer to the California king bed, she saw that the gun was a gold-plated Glock. The magazines, wedged into three other form-fitting compartments, were also gold-plated. She turned to Diego and gave him a questioning look.

"Twenty-four hours a day," he said, loosening his tie, "Seven days a week, I want you to carry that gun everywhere you go. Even when you're with me. No excuses. And I don't mean under the driver's seat or in your glove box. I want it in your purse, with one in the chamber."

Tesla had no issue with toting the gun; she had long ago developed a loving affinity with firearms. But there was something in Diego's tone that worried her. Suddenly she found herself reconsidering Rhonda's ominous warning. Maybe these Mexican cartel thugs who'd kidnapped Diego and his sister when they were kids were back in the picture. Maybe this time they meant to kidnap his girlfriend.

Upon even closer inspection, Tesla saw that there were a number of jewels embedded along the gun's slide and in its handle. She lifted it out of its compartment and pulled back the slide. The chamber was empty. There was no magazine in the butt.

"I like this," she said. "This bitch is sexy. I want it registered in my name."

"It already is."

"Sweet."

She pointed the Glock at the wall of windows across the room from her. All she saw were her and Diego's reflections – her holding the gun in both hands with one eye squeezed shut, him standing with his tie dangling from one hand and his shirt untucked and halfway unbuttoned – but she imagined an enemy standing in her line of fire. She envisaged Tori, the stripper who'd recently told the girls in the locker room at the Strokers that Tesla should have married named her daughter Toyota instead of Ferrari. Tesla and Juicy had caught up with Tori two weeks ago in the parking lot at Strokers and beat her unconsciously, but the beef was far from over.

"I'm getting you another bodyguard too," Diego said. "Someone to work with Big Rick."

"Nuh uh. What the fuck is going on?" Tesla put the gun down and swung around to face him, grabbing her hips and knitting her brow. "Is there something I need to know about? If so you need to tell me right the fuck now, 'cause I ain't with the surprises. Not them kinda surprises."

"No surprises. Just playing it safe." He removed his shirt, tossed it and his tie over the arm of an overstuffed easy chair. He was reaching back to shut the door when Big Rick stuck his head in.

"Tesla – your purse," Big Rick said, and handed the handbag to Diego, who then shut the door and placed the eighty-thousand-dollar Birkin on the seat of the leather easy chair.

There was a gold-plated handgun tucked into the waistband of Diego's trousers, right at the small of his back.

"Seriously, Diego," Tesla persisted. "What's with all the extra security measures? Let me know something."

Diego said nothing. He walked over and placed his gun on the bed-side table. Sat down on the silk comforter and removed his shoes. His arms were long and lean, strong but not overly muscled. The gold Rolex he had on was just one of many out of his vast collection of wristwatches, usually the only kind of jewelry he wore. But this evening was different. Now there was a second piece of jewelry, an initiated gold-and-diamond ring on the little finger of his left hand.

Tesla put her gun back in its compartment, closed the case, and clasped it shut. Which is when she discovered the long rectangular jewelry box. It had been hidden beneath the gun case's lid. She surmised it was just another bracelet, or a watch, or maybe a necklace. She was unimpressed. Diego had just ignored her question – a considerably important question, in her opinion. – and she hated being ignored. She swept the gun case and the jewelry box off the bed and watched them tumble across the floor.

Diego, down to his boxer-briefs now; let out an entertained chuckle. "I see anger management in your future," He said, folding his trousers and getting up from the bed. Two seconds later he was behind Tesla, his hands on her hips, his chin resting in the crack of her right shoulder. "You're really starting to fit the stereotype of the angry black woman."

"Yeah, and your ass is *real* close to fitting the stereotype of my shoe."

He smiled broadly; she saw it in the window's reflection. "Are you setting the scene for some good makeup sex?"

"Shut up and get away from me."

He chuckled his sexy chuckle, then moved her hair aside and pressed his lips to the nape of her neck. A warm, visceral sensation washed through her. "Up and over?" He asked.

This time it was Tesla who gave no answer. She did, however, raise her arms over her head. Diego unzipped the dress, lifted it up and over her head, turned her to face him, and shaved her rearward onto the bed. She was nude save for her jewelry and heels. She folded her arms below her breasts and narrowed her eyes at Diego, but his eyes didn't meet hers. He stood transfixed by the good stuff below her crossed forearms. Her vastly sloping hips. The glistening white diamond in her navel. Her narrow waistline, meaty thighs, and thick vaginal lips. The tattoo of blossoming roses that snaked around her left thigh and curved up her left hip, tapering off at her lower back.

"I hate being ignored, Diego."

"Oh, don't you worry," Diego said, going to his knees beside the bed and hoisting her thighs onto his shoulders. "You have my full attention."

Lazaro Santos sat alone at the exclusive Club Prive in the Bellagio hotel. The private casino was richly appointed in art deco style: dark wood, black lacquer, hung with textured glass and silver screens. The air smelled like the inside of a bank vault.

Laz had been banned from the card tables, but that was okay. He wants her to gamble. From where he sat in the plush armchair, he could see Adela Calderon and Jim Naughton walking toward his table.

Adela was twenty-three, petite, with sun-bronzed skin as smooth as an infant's bottom. Laz had met her when she was serving drinks in the VIP lounge at the Eiffel Tower, Paris Hotel and Casino. This evening, the adorable woman wore an Emilio Pucci red-sequined dress that cost around four thousand dollars, Chanel's latest design of chandelier earrings, and strappy Louis Vuitton sandals, all of which he'd paid for.

The man walking next to her looked much younger than his forty-nine years, had a narrow, intelligent face, curly brown hair, wore a blue suit and glasses with wire rims. Jim Naughton was a former California-based DEA agent who'd lost his badge after it was discovered that he'd been tampering with evidence since the late eighties. He and several other DEA and Border Patrol agents had been on the Mexican drug cartels' payrolls for two decades. They'd worked with all the major cartel bosses: Felix "El Padrino" Gallando in the late eighties, Ramon and Benjamin Arellano Felix throughout the nineties, and now Jaoquin "El Chapo" Guzman, who'd recently take control of the Felix brothers' Tijuana cartel and merged it with his Sinaloa cartel. Laz head learned all this from Uncle Alvaro, who'd supplied the aforementioned Mexican cartel bosses with much of their cocaine since Don Pablo was killed in ninety-four. After being unceremoniously dropped from the DEA and losing the pension he'd worked his ass off for, Naughton had gone into the arms business, opening one Jim's Guns in Houston and another in Dallas.

A waiter walked into Lazaro's view, replacing his empty glass with a new tumbler of Jack Daniel's. When Lazaro could see Jim and Adela again, they were just a few feet from his table, passing the table where Diego's two giant bodyguards, Lee and Max, were seated.

He stood up and reached out to shake Jim's hand. "Evening, Mr. Naughton." They shook hands. Adela gave Lazaro a hug, and the three of them sat down.

Jim leaned forward, beaming. "Pleasure to meet you, Mr. Santos. I must say, I am truly impressed. First-class United flight, luxury car service to the airport in Houston and from the airport here in Vegas." He nodded his head. "Nice."

"Only the best for a potential partner," Lazaro said. "Glad you could make it."

"I'll never turn down a free trip to Las Vegas. Haven't been here since my honeymoon twenty years ago."

Lazaro glanced at Jim Naughton's ringless ring finger.

"She divorced me a year and a half ago when the shit hit the fan," Jim said, catching Lazaro's glance. "Took me for everything. My house, my SUV, half my fucking Beanie Baby collection, my goddam dog. It was a mess, about as acrimonious as a divorce can get. Fucked me royally. I can hardly even visit my kids. Luckily I kept my credit rating together. Bank approved the loans I needed to get my gun stores up and running. Sales are a bit shaky now but we're making progress, getting the company name out there. I'm looking to have a hundred stored all across the South within the next eight or nine years. Ambitious, I know, but that's the plan."

Adela, who had tittered merrily at Jim's mention of a Beanie Baby collection, stopped a passing waiter and ordered a gin and tonic. Jim requested his namesake, a glass of Jim Beam on the rocks.

Lazaro said, "I invited you here for a reason, Mr. Naughton. A damned good one. Got any idea what that reason might be?"

"I've got a pretty good idea." Jim gave his tie a confident tug. "I did some research on you and your family after you called didn't find much on you, but I saw that you're related to Alvaro Santos. Quite frankly, that's all I needed to see. Whether you all are looking to buy me out of franchise my stores, I am completely open to negotiations. Just give me a number."

Lazaro reached into his suit jacket and pulled two packets of bank-fresh hundreds out of his inside pocket. He slid one to Adela, said, "You mind visiting the ladies' room for five minutes? Or hitting the tables?"

"No problem," she said, grinning and thumb nailing through the bills. Her teeth were perfectly straight and veneered. Laz had paid for those too.

The drinks arrived just as Adela was getting up; she took hers and sauntered off to a card table. Lazaro watched her bouncy little ass until she stopped walking. Then, turning his attention back to Jim, he lost the welcoming smile and slid the second packet to the middle of the table.

"You see, Mr. Naughton," he said, leaning forward and placing his elbows on the table, fingers interlaced before him, "I am a man of business just as you are. No need to beat around the bush. In May of nineteen ninety you and your DEA pals discovered a drug tunnel that ran under the southern border from Mexico and into Douglas, Arizona. I want that tunnel. Either that one or one just like it."

A halting, bewildered look washed over Naughton's narrow face. He looked around with vigilant eyes, searching.

"Its no set-up," Lazaro said. "That ten grand is already yours, and there's another nine hundred and ninety thousand dollars where that came from. A million dollars for access to an out-of-use tunnel. Don't tell me you can't get it done because I got all my information from the other side of the border."

"This is nonsense. I came here to talk business –"

"And we're talking business. Big business,' Lazaro said sharply. "I'll make it two million, but that's my final offer. Call up agents Vosco, McMillan, Gibson, Crump, Perez, Norman. Yeah, I know all about your deal with the Sinaloa cartel. Not that I care one way or another. All I want is for my product to pass through one of those tunnels, and for your boys to look the other way. You help me do that and I'll make sure your hundred-store goal is a success."

For a moment Jim Naughton just stared at Lazaro. Finally, he took a red ink pen from his breast pocket and scribbled something on a napkin. He turned the napkin so Lazaro could read it:

How do I know you're not wired?

Lazaro leaned closer, said, "You told El Padrino that it was Kiki Camarena who'd infiltrated his cartel. You're the reason DEA agent Enrique 'Kiki' Camarena got all the bones in his face broken before El Padrino's top hitman put a hole in his temple with a fucking power drill. If I were a fed, you'd be in ADX right now, not sitting here contemplating a two-million-dollar deal."

Up until this point neither Lazaro nor Jim had lifted their drinks. Now Jim raised his and swallowed half of it in one gulp. He became thoughtful, slowly and jerkily twisting his glass on a coaster, gazing down into the iced liquor. He poured a few drops onto the napkin he'd written his question on then tore it to shreds, his jaw muscles flexing as he clenched and unclenched his teeth. He had long fingers, hairy hands. The narrow strip of skin where his wedding band had once resided was lighter than the rest of his tanned white ring finger.

"How much was Joaquin paying you?" Lazaro asked, after a time. "Couldn't have been much. I'll go out on a limb and say five grand a month was doled out to you and each of your crooked DEA buddies. Most of your share was probably used to put your daughter through law school, and what was left you spent traveling the world with your dear ex-wife and sprucing up that nice rustic Texas ranch she took in the divorce. Now all that good drug money's gone. You're up to your throat in debt, stretched thin by two underperforming businesses, and since you're no longer a federal agent, those monthly payments from the Sinaloa Cartel are a thing of the past. Admit it, Jim. You need me more than I need you."

"Let's say I do. How do I know you won't have someone put a bullet in my head once you have the tunnel?"

"Because it wouldn't benefit me. The tunnel would be raided by your DEA pals and I'd be stuck without a way in."

Jim was silent for a long moment. "That hole in Douglas was cemented in fifteen years ago," he said finally.

"Then get me another one."

Jim stood up, finishing off his drink as he rose from the armchair. Lazaro pushed the packet of hundred toward Jim, and Jim snatched it up. He flicked through the bills.

"Okay," he said. "Give me a week. I have to meet with some people fact to face. I'll call you with an answer next week."

"No. You'll *meet* with me next week, and you'll bring directions to a tunnel," Lazaro replied, standing up. "Our first phone call was out last. I'll have a car sent to pick you up from your Houston business next Friday at noon."

Jim reached out and they shook hands.

"See you next week," he said.

"Plata o plomo," Lazaro replied, stone-faced.

The Spanish-to-English translation "Plata o plomo" was "Silver of Lead," Which meant a person had the choice of either accepting a bribe or taking a bullet.

Tesla was stroking her fingers through Diego's short dark hair. Her face was fixed in a look of passionate confusion, as though she could not understand how his tongue and fingers were capable of giving her so much pleasure. Brow furrowed, mouth agape, she stared down at his rapidly moving tongue, watching it do laps around her clitoris while he pistoned two fingers in and out of her sopping-wet pussy.

Diego couldn't help but smile, not only because he absolutely loved the taste and smell of her but also because she was no longer pissed at him for ignoring her questions. He'd successfully broken through the wall she always threw up when things didn't go her way. All it took was a good tongue-lashing.

He knew that she was nearing a second orgasm when her breaths quickened and she started humping at his mouth. He separated the two fingers he had inside of her, stretching her open, she clamped her hands onto sides of his head, holding his hungrily licking mouth tight against her engorged clit, winding her glorious brown hips, grinding her pussy on his tongue. She let go of his head and filled her palms with her soft, natural breasts. She gave voice to a shrieking falsetto of great erotic means. Her flawless body jerked and trembled spasmodically as a powerful climax ripped through her. Her bubbly white vaginal juices flowed out over Diego's steadily prodding fingers.

Rising to his socked feet, Diego freed his erection from his black Calvin Klein boxer-briefs; at eighteen he had become a Calvin Klein underwear model, and although he'd given up his modeling career shortly thereafter, he still preferred to wear CK underwear.

His penis was four inches long, flaccid and about seven and a half inches long erect, and it curved downward. Heather Modine, the Dominican porn star he'd dated before Tesla, had told him that the peculiar curve of his dick made it easy to deep throat because it fit the arch of her throat perfectly. He had no pubic hair; Heather had insisted on him being clean-shaven down there, and he'd kept it that way ever since.

He walked over to the nightstand and picked up a ribbed Trojan condom. "Up on all fours," he said. "Now. I'm gonna cure you of that attitude."

Tesla giggled weakly. "Boy, my whole bottom half is shaking like I got Parkinson's right now." She was on her side, balled up like a baby in the womb.

"I don't care. You threw those boxes on the *floor*, gifts I used my hard-earned money to pay for. Every action has a reaction. Didn't you learn that in grammar school?" He put the condom on as he returned to where he'd kneeled a moment prior. Tesla hadn't moved, so he rolled her over and shoved her knees up under her.

"So *aggressive*," she said.

Diego gave her left buttock a hard smack, then stepped forward and sank his dick into her slippery pussy. He clamped his strong, veiny hands on her hips and went in deep. Balls deep. The sound of Tesla sucking in a breath lifted the right side of his mouth and formed his idiosyncratic grin.

He began pounding in and out of her, subconsciously taking out his anger on her tight, noisily wet pussy, which had suddenly become a vicarious sacrifice for Sofia's coldly inflammatory remarks.

Diego had ordered his pilot to steer his Gulfstream straight to the Las Vegas airport. To hell with Sofia; she could fly commercials. She was probably sitting in the first-class section on an American Airlines flight at this very moment, pouting, thinking mean thoughts. Or maybe her flight had already landed at the Los Angeles airport and she was now wrapped up in Emilio's athletic arms, telling him about the threat Diego had made against his left arm. Whatever the case, Diego was not sympathetic.

During the first hour of the three-hour flight from Barranquilla to Vegas, Diego and Lazaro had discussed several ways to smuggle a large shipment of cocaine into the United States. Their cartel supplied bricks of coke to just about every drug cartel in Mexico, but Colombians were merely the producers, the wholesalers. The average price of a kilogram from the Barranquilla Cartel was $5,500; the

Mexican Cartels normally sold each kilo to their American counterparts for $14,000 to $18,000 and the North American's sold the kilos for $19,000 to $28,000.

Diego wanted to cut out the Mexican drug cartels. He was confident that he could be as big of a Colombian drug lord as his infamous godfather Don Pablo, who had sold kilos of cocaine in the United States for $70,000.

Diego's thrusts were rabbit fast. Tesla winced and moaned and crawled halfway across the huge bed; Diego stayed with her, walking on his knees, his pelvis smacking rapidly against her large, bouncing ass. Tesla quivered her way through a third orgasm, then a fourth, and a few minutes after that Diego shot a copious load into the condom. He remained balls deep in her creamy center until his dick stopped twitching, then delivered a final smack to her soft left buttock and watched her thick legs slide out from under her.

He padded into the bathroom, flushed the condom, stripped off his socks, watch, and underwear, and stepped into the vast shower stall. It had a lot of shower heads, a marble floor, and a glass wall, similar to the master bath at his Stone Mountain estate. He turned on the water and let the showerheads beat down on his body.

Tesla joined him in the shower a moment later.

"So," She asked, squeezing a dollop of fragrant body wash on a loofah, "How'd the funeral go? Is your mom okay?"

"She's fine," Diego said. "Distraught, as you might expect, and drunk as a damn sailor, but fine nonetheless. All her relatives flew in from Brazil. I got to see all my cousins from Niteroi and Rio de Janeiro. Hadn't seen them in years."

"What happened over there – *down* there, I mean – that got you all worried about our safety? It had to be something. Don't worry about me getting scared or no shit like that. I'm a project chick; only thing scare me is a disloyal friend."

Tesla was soaping up her tits, gazing up at Diego with her intoxicating eyes. Her skin, reddish brown and silky smooth, was a thing of beauty. Her dark nipples peeked through the bubbly white suds. Looking at her took away Diego's worries and made him less nervous about the implicit power that came with his newly acquired piranha ring.

"It's my sister," he said, after a contemplative moment. "Sofia's not too fond of our relationship. I can't risk leaving you unprotected while she and I are on bad terms. She's a lot more dangerous than she looks. The fact that she doesn't like you only exacerbates that danger. When I was sixteen, she had my girlfriend Sara murdered in a brazen drive-by on South Beach. We need to take precautionary measures – to be on the safe side, you know."

Tesla rolled her pretty eyes. "If you think I'm about to be scared of some skinny-ass model bitch, you got me confused with the next bitch. This ain't that. I wouldn't give a damn who she did or didn't like. Dee, you better check that bitch. I will beat the brakes off that girl. She better check my background."

"This is different."

"I'm different."

"I'm serious, Tesla. This is no fighting matter. She'll turn your life upside down if she comes after you. She'll do everything in her power to ruin you personally, socially, and financially, and then she'll send in the goons."

Chapter 5

Enzo's unique ride was a 1969 Oldsmobile Cutlass that boasted red candy paint, black racing stripes, a black leather Gucci top, and a shiny set of 24-inch Lexani rims. Numerous televisions and eardrum-punishing speakers were installed throughout the sleek cherry convertible. The interior had plush basket seats upholstered in black leather with red stitching. The engine and pipes were all chromed out. The windows and seats were electronically powered, and there was a twelve-disk CD changer that Enzo kept stocked with his favorite rappers' latest and greatest albums and mixtapes. Enzo loved his Cutlass almost as much as he loved his three beautiful daughters, though neither of the three were allowed to eat or drink inside of it.

The time was 2:02 am Enzo was standing next to his car in the parking lot of strip club on Moreland Avenue, smoking a Newport cigarette and sipping form a red plastic solo cup of Remy Martin VSOP. he wore a thick red Nautica hoodie, matching sweatpants, black and red Air Force one sneakers. His nose, lips, and hands were cold, though not unbearably, and his eyes were peeled for Debbie, the stripper he'd been fucking for the past few weeks.

The name of the strip club was Blazin' Saddles, and the parking lot was packed. Enzo's car was dope, but it paled in comparison to some of the others. Jeezy and his BMF crew were gathered around a fleet of Lamborghinis, Ferraris, and Rolls-Royces, getting ready to leave. And there were others:

a silver Mercedes on nice chrome rims, an orange Bentley coupe, two new model Jaguars, a dozen older-model whips like Enzo's on twenty-twos and twenty-fours. Blaze was one of East Atlanta's more popular strip clubs, a place where a lot of high rollers showed up to show out.

Parked next to Enzo's convertible was a beautiful red 1996 Chevy Impala SS with darkly tinted windows and 24-inch spinning rims. The Impala belonged to Keyvon, Enzo's close friend. They'd met in Fulton County jail, but they hadn't become partners until they landed in the same prison together. A knife fight with a set of Crips from Savannah had solidified their bond. Keyvon Gail, who went by the nickname Kilo, was twenty-three, same age as Enzo, and they were both MOB Piru Bloods.

Kilo emerged from the crowd of BMF members and strode toward Enzo. he was also smoking and drinking, only his smoke was a blunt of dro and his red plastic cup had Lean in it. He was short and brown-skinned, muscular, and arrogant. He had sixteen gold teeth with diamonds in them, a bald head, a cross tatted between his eyebrows, and two red teardrops tatted next to his right eye. He motioned for Enzo to join him in the Impala; Enzo pulled open the passenger door and got in.

"I hollered at Blu," Kilo said. "He talkin' nineteen-five a piece, say he'll give us four whole thangs if we give him half the bread up front."

"You tell him we want 'em?"

"Hell yeah. He says give him an hour. He gon' have his bitch bring 'em to the Knights Inn. we good, blood." Kilo tapped his blunt over the ashtray. "How much you got on you?"

"Fourteen thousand. Had to borrow twenty-five hundred from my uncle."

"Damn, how much you put in the Cutlass?"

"Too much. Eight thousand on the rims and tires. Twenty on the engine. That's what really fucked me up. Plus, I had to pay for the lift kit, new brake pads, and the stash box. Not to mention all the shit I bought my daughter for her party."

"Don't even trip, blood. I'll pay the difference."

"You know I'm good for it."

"Already."

Enzo wrestled a huge rubber-banded pile of cash out of his right-hand pocket and another out of his left. "That's the whole fourteen," he said, handing the cash over to Kilo. "I'll get the other fifty-five hundred from Debbie if Bo ain't got it by the time we get back to the trap."

"I ain't worried about that lil change. Juicy gave me ten thousand before she went to Vegas the other night. From what she told me earlier, you need to be tryna get in good with Tesla. Ya girl got a billionaire boyfriend. The nigga got hi sown private jet, and she say his daddy got ties to a Colombian drug cartel. We need in on that."

"Tess ain't fuckin' wit' me no more," Enzo said dejectedly. He smashed his cigarette out in the ashtray, set his cup in the cup holder, and gritted his teeth as his dejection gave way to indignation. "That bitch – I swear, blood, I wanna smack the fuck out that bitch. She ain't gave me shit but ten racks since I came home. Ten thousand dollars. I used to give her ten racks every weekend just to go shoppin' and get her hair and nails done. You know how much money I blew on that bitch before I caught that case? Her first car was a CLK 430 Benz and guess who paid for it? Me. Her second car was a Lexus SC430, and guess who paid for it. I did. I asked her for some money a few hours ago, and this bitch had the nerve to tell me she'll see what she can do. I hung up on her dog ass. Bitch got me fucked up."

"You gotta sweet talk her, bruh. Shit, you cheated and had a baby by her best friend from fourth grade. She ain't about to just get over that. You gotta work your way back in, apologize to her, tell her you regret all the bullshit you put her through, tell her you were too young and dumb to understand how wrong the shit was when you did it. Take out all that anger and put in some strategy."

Enzo ran a hand down his face. He picked up his cup and took a swallow. It was difficult to admit, but he knew that Kilo was right. He'd committed the ultimate betrayal when he started fucking Stacy Garrett, a girl who'd been one of Tesla's best friends until he got her pregnant the same month he got Tesla pregnant.

"You got good taste, though," Kilo said smilingly. Tendrils of smoke swelled up from both ends of his blunt. "Stacy, a bad bitch. Debbie is a bad bitch. Tesla is the baddest bitch in the city. Your other baby-mama bad as fuck. All you gotta do now is get rich. Stay focused on that bread. Make sure that when Tesla sees you back on top, she ain't gon' have no choice but to forgive you and give you some money, some pussy, some jewelry. Some *everything*. This our year, blood. We gon' fuck shit up this summer, whether Tesla help you or not."

Enzo was nodding his head thoughtfully, really imbibing Kilo's sage advice, when Debbie and another stripper came sauntering their way. He shoved open his door and got out. He didn't realize how warm it had been inside the Impala until the cold air outside hit him like a glacier shot from a cannon.

He tossed his empty cup and smiled a mouthful of gold teeth; his had no diamonds in them, but all thirty-two of them were gold.

Debbie and her stripper colleague were clad in form-fitting high-end designer sweatshirts over tight jeans and exclusive Jordan sneakers, and they were carrying black plastic trash bags, fat ones that Enzo knew were stuffed with one-dollar bills. The friend, who looked to be several years older than twenty-year-old Debbie, went to the silver S550 Benz that was parked two spaces to the right of Enzo's car and tossed her bags – the trash bag and a duffel – in the back seat. He popped his trunk for Debbie, ignoring the fact that she and her friend were staring across the lot at Jeezy's crew.

"All those cars are leased," Debbie said, placing her duffel and trash bag in the trunk. She was a short girl, just four foot eleven, and she weighed about a hundred forty pounds. Her hair was colored blond and cut extremely short, though all of it was covered beneath her Rockets skullcap. She had soft, thick lips, reddish brown skin, and the kind of fat, round, fluffy derriere that had long ago become a prerequisite for any woman who wished to date Enzo. unclipping her cell phone from the Chanel purse hanging under her arm, she said, "Shanita's auntie works at the luxury car dealership where Jay got that Lambo. He only had to put down ten percent of the MSRP, which was twenty-one thousand and some change. He pays about two thousand dollars a month. Can you believe that? I'm about to start saving up to get me a Bentley."

"Nah," Enzo said, shutting the trunk and walking her to the passenger door, "Fuck a Bentley. Finish up in college first. Get those degrees. A Bentley ain't gon' do shit for your kids." He opened the passenger door, waited for her to get comfortably seated, and then shut the door and walked around the front of the car to the driver's side.

He was being a hypocrite. Since his release from prison he'd put at least seventy grand into the Cutlass. The truth of the matter was that he didn't want Debbie to outshine him. He wanted her to essentially become his second source of income. He needed jewelry, another Mercedes, a big house in the exurbs, and a studio to record his music.

Most importantly, he needed more cocaine.

He got in behind the wheel, started the engine.

"You're right," Debbie said in a low, defeated tone. "I can't pull up to Spelman in a Bentley. Not while I got Natavia and Jamari staying with my mama. I need to put them first. Indeed to get my priorities in order, get ten or fifteen thousand saved up so I can get a nice house and get my babies moved in with me."

"Eyes on the prize," Enzo concurred. He was easing his top-up convertible out of the parking lot ahead of Kilo, chucking up the deuces to a few old associates, flashing smiles at the women who still wanted to fuck him because they thought he was still rolling in money.

"I admit," Debbie said, pouring herself a cup of Remy. "I do lose sight of what I'm here for every now and then. It's hard seeing all these ball players and street niggas with big diamond watches and necklaces on, throwing ten and twenty thousand dollars in singles at a bitch every time they hit the club and then driving off in Lambos and Rolls-Royces. You don't see that where I come from. I mean, you see it, but not in my hood. Not in the Fifth Ward. Benz and Jags, you see those, but you'll never see a Rolls-Royce Phantom on Liberty Road. You'd have to go to the other side of Houston to see that."

"You'll get there soon enough. Be patient."

"You should see if your baby-mama Tesla can get me in one of those music videos. She's the hottest thing in Atlanta right now. On the female side, I mean. She's in, like, seven of the top ten videos on 106th and Park. Shanita saw her pull up to Club 112 last weekend in a clean-ass Ferrari. They say she blew fifteen g's in the VIP section, bought all kinds of bottles, smoked out everybody – the whole shebang. The other two bitches she was with hopped out a Range Rover. She even had Big Rick, Usher's old bodyguard, as her personal security."

"Yeah, she done came up. I'm glad for her," Enzo lied. "We'll get you to that same level one day. It took Tesla years to get to that level."

"Well, where do we start?"

"Just keep doing you. Keep networking and dancing and sooner or later you'll meet the right people. When you do, give 'em my number and tell 'em they gotta talk to your manager. I'm working on getting you in some magazines now. Been on the phone all day."

Debbie gasped. "Really?!"

Enzo nodded. In truth, he hadn't spoken with anyone about getting Debbie into any magazine, but she leaned in and planted a big smacky kiss on his cheek as if she truly believed him. He vowed to himself that he would at least make some inquiries after the weekend, see what steps it would take to get Debbie into the urban modeling game. He really did want her to win. Hell, he needed her to win.

"I was talking with some of the girls," Debbie said tentatively. "Don't flip out on me, okay? It's just an idea."

"It better be about some money."

"Oh, it's definitely about some money. I wouldn't bring it up if it wasn't."

"What is it?"

Debbie hesitated. She took a deep breath and let it out. She picked at the lip of her cup. "How would you feel about me getting into the ... the adult film industry?" She said finally. "I hear the pay is really good," she added.

"Porn?" Enzo's eyebrows came together. They were idling behind a beat-to-shit Ford sedan, waiting on the red-light to go dark and the green light to show its pleasant face. Enzo had the heat blowing hard, a UGK track playing at low volume, the movie Paid In Full playing on all ten of his TV screens. He looked over at Debbie; smiling nervously, she avoided his curious stare. "You mean porn?" He asked again.

Debbie nodded sheepishly.

Just then, a dark-colored older model Suburban came to a screeching halt on Debbie's side of the car. The doors were open before the SUV had even stopped, all four of them. All four of the men who rushed out of the SUV were wearing black ski-masks. Two of them had handguns with extended magazines, one guy had a submachine gun, and the fourth man brandished an AK-47.

They trained their guns on the Cutlass and the Impala sitting behind it.

There was no time for Enzo to reach for the nine-millimeter he had stashed under his seat, so he raised his hands in surrender. Debbie yelped, and her cup slipped from her hand and hit the floorboard.

The man with the AK-47 circled around to Enzo's door. "Put it in park and get the fuck out," he shouted, snatching the door open.

Enzo shifted into park. "Just get out," he said to Debbie. His heart was pummeling his ribcage. As much as he wanted to resist, he knew that he had to step out and give up the car. It was nice and all, but it wasn't worth dying over.

He put one leg out and started to stand, but before he could rise out of his seat he was snatched out of the car and thrown to the ground. His waistline and pockets were frisked, his wallet and cigarettes confiscated. Debbie shrieked as she was thrown down beside him and robbed of her purse and jewelry. He looked to his left and saw that Kilo was also lying face-down in the middle of the street, the AK barrel resting on the nape of his neck while another gunman raided his pockets.

A volcanic rage bubbled up from Enzo's core, fueling him with adrenaline. The urge to react heroically became almost too overwhelming, but it was an urge he had to repress. Unarmed, he didn't stand a chance against the four gunmen, who raced away seconds later, taking the Cutlass and Kilo's Impala with them and leaving Kilo and Enzo lying in the middle of the street with their pockets turned inside out.

Chapter 6

Just over three hours after its departure from the Las Vegas airport, the Gulfstream touched down on the tarmac in Atlanta so smoothly it felt like they'd landed in a field of silk. Or maybe it was the Hennessy, already numbing Tesla's senses, coloring everything wonderful. Wonderful is what she had been promised, and so far Diego had delivered marvelously.

"We are back in the A, bitch!" Tesla announced to the group, taking the last swallow of her cognac and pumping her fist in the air.

"Two nights away was long enough for me," Rhonda said from her reclined chair.

Juicy, seated across from Tesla in the spacious cabin, picked up her empty glass and tossed her long blond hair. "Bitch, I'm about to call up Keyvon and get me some dick. That triple-stack got me horny as fuck. I let the lil Boston nigga eat me out, but he couldn't even get that right. Lickin' all in the hole and shit. I was like Dude, that hole is for fingers and dick. You're not even supposed to be licking way down there – not unless you're licking my asshole. Lick the fucking clit. Pull the hood back and lick on the little beacon, the little man in the boat."

Rhonda, whose features had shifted into a grimace of disgust the moment Juicy mentioned getting her asshole licked, said, "You've actually had your asshole licked? I knew you were nasty and all, but that's just disgusting."

Tesla and Juicy exploded with laughter. Rollicking, gut-clenching, doubled-over laughter. Rhonda laughed too, though her disgusted expression remained intact.

"I'm missing my baby," Tesla said when the laughter subsided. "Gotta have mama come and drop her off to me asap."

"Yeah, I miss my lil badass babies too," Juicy said, her disingenuous tone making it comically obvious that she didn't miss her little badass babies at all.

The time in Atlanta was 9:15 am. Tesla and her girls hadn't slept a wink, but Diego and Lazaro were fast asleep, as were the three bodyguards. Shortly after Tesla and Diego had finished showering, Juicy and Rhonda had returned to the Blue Sky Villa with a baggie of ecstasy pills Juicy got from one of the Boston boys. The pills were triple-stacked Blue. dolphins, which meant they packed three times the punch. They'd each swallowed a pill before packing their bags and heading out for the airport. Tesla's pill had kicked in almost immediately, and she'd been on cloud nine ever since.

"I swear," Juicy said, her thumb pounding away at the buttons on her Nextel, "Keyvon got me soooo fucked up right now. This nigga ain't answered none of my text messages, and his phone keeps sending me to voicemail."

"Maybe he's sleeping like most normal people are at this hour," Rhonda suggested.

"No. he would've told me he was going to go to bed if that was the case."

"Then maybe he's getting – or giving – some head like you were last night."

Juicy looked up from her phone and gave Rhonda a frigid stare.

Tesla checked her own cell phone. She'd sent Enzo a text three hours ago letting him know that she was on her way back to Atlanta and that he could come and get the money he needed from her mother's apartment at around noon. (She had not given him the address to Diego's palatial Stone Mountain estates, and she strictly forbade anyone else from doing so). She found it odd that Enzo hadn't replied to her text. He was usually awake until around this time. He had to have seen her text by now.

"Knowing Enzo," Tesla said, getting up and putting on her fifty-thousand-dollar chinchilla coat, "They're probably somewhere laid up with some bitches we call friends."

"That's another possibility," Rhonda added cheerfully.

"I hate both of you bitches," Juicy said.

Tesla woke the man with a single shrill shout. Ten minutes later they deplaned. The trio of brawny black bodyguards piled into a waiting SUV after the rest of them climbed into a chauffeured black Hummer limo that whisked them away from Hartsfield-Jackson International and into the heart of Atlanta.

Diego pressed a button that converted the rearmost seats to a bed. He lay on the bed with his head nestled in Tesla's lap, Lazaro with his head nestled in Rhonda's.

Juicy laughed and said, "That's about as close to getting some head as Rhonda will ever get."

Rhonda raised a middle finger and presented it to Juicy. Tesla and Juicy snickered merrily. This was Lazaro's fourth time being around Rhonda, and just like the last three times, he was as close to her as he could possibly be. The sexual tension was palpable. Lazaro fell back to sleep with a devious grin on his face.

The girls began making phone calls and sending text messages. Tesla called her mom first and told her she was back in Atlanta, and also that the Church Street house was ready to be moved into.

"Good," Claudia said. "I was about ready to lose my damn mind. I'm so sick of these projects. Everybody thinks I got money because of you. I got all kinds of new friends. Fake love is the worst love. Don't you ever forget it."

"Mama, you could've moved out the projects a long time ago. You're only there because you chose to stay there."

"You tried to move me out there around them white folks. I told you, I'm not leaving the wet side for nobody. I made my bones right here in Zone 1, and this is where I'm staying till – hold on." She shouted a threat at Marlon's two-year-old daughter Marlana, told the little girl she'd wring her neck if she broke that ashtray. "I'ma strangle this lil heifer. Her daddy better hurry up and get outta jail before I end up in there with him."

The things Mama Cece said when she was frustrated.

Tesla tittered. "Mama, you need meds."

"Damn right I do. Some hydro. Some chromic."

"Have you heard from Lorenzo?"

"Nope. Donny says he got robbed sometime last night, though. He and the same thing from Stacy."

Tesla gasped. "Robbed?"

"Mm hm. Carjacked and robbed at gunpoint. One of Donny's nephews saw him leaving Blaze in that red Cutlass. He wasn't far from Blaze when they got him. Jacked his boy Kilo too."

Wide-eyed and thunderstruck, Tesla relayed the news to Juicy, whose eyes got just as big as she looked up from her phone.

"They took his phone," Claudia went on. "He used somebody else's to call Stacy. She went and picked him up at around three o'clock this morning, took him and Kilo to some stripper's apartment right off Windsor, over there in Zone 3. She stopped by and told me all about it before she went to work a few hours ago, and said Lorenzo was 'bout ready to kill somebody."

"You know it's about to go down, mama. Damn near the whole Bowen Homes gon' ride for Zo."

"They're already cliqued up and outside, a whole gang of 'em. Want me to bring Rari to you? Because I 'm ready to get a U-Haul and get outta here today, and I don't need no kids getting all in my way."

"I'll be home in about thirty minutes. Just bring her to me."

"You sure my house is ready to be –"

"Yes, Ma, I'm absolutely sure. Diego told me when we got to the airport in Vegas. The people who renovated the house are the same guys he uses to renovate his luxury properties. You'll be the only person in Bankhead with Italian marble floors and high-tech security cameras. Let me call Ms. Hollis and make sure Zo's okay."

"Okay, call me back."

Instead of phoning Lorenzo's mother, Tesla sent texts to his mother, his two sisters and his uncle Joe. While she awaited their reply, she phoned Lea; a girl she knew who danced at Blaze. She didn't get an answer.

Looking up at Juicy Tesla said, "Call Stacy and ask that dirty bitch who she dropped Zo off with. Ask her for the address."

Rhonda said, "He's with Debra Hicks." She folded her Nextel shut. "Her stage name is Debbie Cakes. We just call her Debbie."

Tesla swung her head a few degrees and gave Rhonda a short, quizzical look. "Who the fuck is Debra Hicks?"

"She's a girl I go to school with, dances at Blaze, just moved her from Houston a few months ago. I texted her and didn't get an answer, but I know it's her. She started at Spelman last month. Her cousin Quincy lives in those apartments on Glenn Street in Zone 3. She's staying with him until she can find her own place. We talked about it right before we went on spring break last week. She told me she had just started dating some boy from the Westside of Atlanta who had just got out of prison. She didn't say his name but she gave a description that fit Lorenzo to a T. She said he was tall and dark-skinned, tatted up, mouthful of golds. I didn't connect it to Zo until now."

Tesla had more to add to the conversation – the jealous bitch in her wanted to know everything there was to know about Debra Hicks – but out of respect for Diego she minded her inquiring mind and said, "Well, we know they're okay. That's all that matters. Juicy, you knew where to find your man. I'm out of it."

Juicy rolled her eyes, shook her head, and silently mouthed, "So phony." Rhonda grinned and nodded her head in agreement. They both knew the truth of the matter, a truth that was loved by them and loathed by Tesla.

The loathed truth was, there were some things in life that were hard to let go, and the love Tesla had for Lorenzo Hollis was one of them.

Diego sat up as soon as his hummer limo passed through the monogrammed wrought iron gates at the forefront of his three-acre Stone Mountain estate. He felt well-rested. He slept on the flight from Barranquilla to Vegas and again on the flight from Vegas to Atlanta.

"Morning, sleepyhead," Tesla said, and planted a kiss on his cheek. She was wearing the hundred-thousand dollar diamond necklace shed' thrown to the floor in the bedroom of their hotel suite last night. A shimmery glass gave her soft, full lips the appearance of being perpetually wet. Her verdant green eyes were dilated, and Diego wondered whether it was ecstasy or coke Juicy had convinced her to take this time.

He hoped it was ecstasy.

Tesla was a full-blown nymphomaniac on ecstasy.

Flanked by low, neatly groomed hedges and bronze statues of lions, tigers, and cheetahs, the Graystone drive leading up to the main house was smooth and wide. The driveway opened into a vast rectangular parking area, large enough for twenty vehicles and continued on into a carport that could fit six more. A Graystone guardhouse stood at the west end of the parking area. An armed guard stepped out and eyed the blacked-out limo and the blacked-out SUV behind it as they cruised up the drive and into the carport.

Diego had purchased the estate from the owner of the Atlanta Falcons. Then he'd pumped a few million into various improvements – most of it sucked into the grotto and waterfall system he had added to the enclosed swimming pool behind the main house and the remainder sucked into the state-of-the-art guardhouse and security system. The guardhouse was manned twenty-four hours a day by four armed bodyguards, all of whom were Colombian-Americans imported from Miami to safeguard the estate. Each camera was connected to a motion sensor and floodlight, creating an impenetrable ring of security.

They climbed out of the limo – Diego, Lazaro, and Tesla, who told Rhonda and Juicy she'd catch up with them later. The limo backed out into the parking area, turned around, and drove down the driveway and out the still open gates as Diego led the way into the main house through the breezeway. The bodyguards were seconds behind, wheeling in their suitcases and handing them over to Diego and Tesla's eccentric caterie of domestic help.

The eccentric coterie included four pleasantly plump, Spanish-speaking maid, two of whom had been picking up after Diego since he was a toddler; a garrulous Jamaican nanny, Dotty, who was running up a thousand-dollar-a-month phone bill, calling her family in Kingston; a black electrician from Brooklyn, who was always sneaking hot young debentures into the guest house; a pale white handyman, who had a nasty scar on the side of his face and only three fingers on his left hand, the result of an insane machete attack outside a bar Alvaro Santos owned in Bogota, Colombia; Diego's personal maid, Claire, who anticipated his every need as if she could read minds; the armed guards, who kept out the thieves and robbers; four full-time landscapers, one of which had recently been bitten by Diego's snow-white French bulldog, Diamante, who bit anyone who dared go within three feet of Rari's bedroom door, especially when Rari was in a pouty mood; Diego's personal chief, Pari, a Pakistani immigrant who behaved more like his mother than his cook; and the most recent addition to the caterie – three full-time cosmetologists, two for Tesla's hair (and Diego's whenever he needed a cut), one for her makeup and nails, all of whom would be traveling with Pari from Vegas in the first-class section of an American Airlines passenger jet whenever they woke up. And then, of course, there was Leroy Rigney, Diego's coal-black driver, who had done twenty-three years in a Georgia prison for a murder conviction and acted as if every non-black person he encountered was an undercover cop looking to put him behind bars, even Diego.

Claire took Diego's pea coat and Tesla's fur as they traipsed through the massive, marble-floored foyer. Diamante appeared from behind a gray marble pillar and came running at his owners. Not much bigger than a kitten, Diamante was a chubby little dog, always bustling with energy. He ran circles around them as they entered the parlor, barking excitedly. Diego reached down and gave the fat little dog a pat on the side of the belly, then sat down in his favorite overstuffed armchair, eyeing Tesla's vastly rounded derriere as she sauntered across the custom-made taupe and white $140,000 Edward Fields carpet. Her fifty-thousand-dollar diamond hoop earrings swung gently on either side of her perfect face. The jade green Prada dress she had on fit her like a second skin, and it accentuated her blazing green eyes. She was already on her cell phone, jabbering to someone about an upcoming club event. She bent and scooped up Diamante, dodged his thick pink tongue, then turned and left the room.

Lazaro sat in the armchair across the coffee table from Diego. "Were you being serious when you threatened to maim Emilio? Should I send someone to watch him? Have him followed?"

"How many men do we have here in the Atlanta area?" Diego asked.

"We've got, uh … twenty or so. Twenty-one. Seven at each stash house. Why?"

"I want that number to triple in the coming weeks. Start the vetting process."

Lazaro nodded, then tilted his head back against the soft taupe. Italian leather and closed his eyes. In Spanish, he said, "Sofia may have had a point. I overheard the girls talking on the way here. Seemed to me like Tesla was more concerned about her ex than she should be. He got carjacked and robbed. Tesla got all worked up about it."

Diego's face became fixed in a grim expression, as if he were suppressing some profound emotion. "Let's stay focused. There's a lot of money to be made here. Billions. Give me ideas, not gossip." He lifted his legs onto the leather ottoman in front of his armchair, crossed them at the ankles. "Contact the Ruiz brothers in Chicago, and our Haitian friends in Miami. Make sure they're ready to do business. $14,000-a-kilo, just like last time. Purest coke they'll ever taste. I want those kilos gone before they're even here. What can Adela do to help us this go around?"

"She knows all the kingpins. There's a new kid in D.C. who moves over a hundred kilos per week. Name's Bundy. They're calling him the new Rayful Edmond. He hit the Bellagio with an entourage of about twenty guys just last week and gambled away over a million dollars. Didn't lose a wink of sleep over it. Adela's seen him do it several times over the past few months. There's another guy in Harlem, a girl in Charlotte, North Carolina, a pair of cousins in Cincinnati, Ohio, a former NFL player in Indianapolis, a Dominican gang leader in Philadelphia. Same deal with all of them. Big-time cake dealers who choose to blow their dough around sin City every now and then. Adela has all their phone numbers. She should be in D.C. to speak with Bundy by noon Eastern."

"We received the confirmation email from Lagos. The Nigerians have the shipment, and they wired the ten million to your Cayman Island account."

Diego nodded his head, grinning triumphantly. For years the Barranquilla Cartel had been sending coke stashed in shipping containers from South America to Lagos, Nigeria, flooding West Africa with piranha-stamped bricks of cocaine that were subsequently dispersed throughout the continent and smuggled into Europe. The ten million U.S. dollars wired from Lagos was payment for a thousand kilos of coke that had been concealed in a shipment of Colombian coffee.

"Imagine if we could fill up one of those shipping containers and get it into the States," Diego said thoughtfully.

"We did that twice last year."

"Yeah, but we didn't fill up an entire container. We got fifteen hundred kilos in one container, fifteen hundred in another, and forty-five hundred kilos in that piece of shit submarine that sank off the Baja Peninsula on the journey back from San Diego. I want a whole container full of coke."

"Coast Guard sank that sub," Lazaro said.

"That's speculation." Diego began twisting and tugging on his piranha ring. "How many kilos do you think can fit in one of those shipping containers?"

"Each shipping container can hold up to a hundred tons," Lazaro said with a notable sigh. "Twenty-seven hundred containers on every ship. About seventy-five hundred of them are unloaded at the Port of New Jersey every day."

Claire walked in with a tray that held a bottle of cold Fiji water and two glass tumblers. She was a woman of about fifty. She had shoulder-length, gray-and-black hair, thick and rich, which swept down over her wide forehead in what people called a bang. She had dark brown skin, regular features, heavy breasts, and a sensual, full-lipped mouth but most people only noticed her eyes. She had deep-set, intense eyes of a startling golden hue, so luminous and penetrating that when she looked at you, you felt she could see right into your thoughts, and you averted your eyes, afraid that she would read your mind and discover your deepest secrets. She was wearing the customary black blouse and black skirt, Manolo Blahnik flats, and the pearl necklace Diego had gifted her last Christmas.

She filled the two glasses with water, placed them on coasters on the coffee table, and left the room. Diego picked up his tumbler and took a drink, a thousand yard stare fixed on his face as he imagined himself successfully smuggling a hundred tons of uncut cocaine into the United States in a shipping container.

"A hundred tons of blow," he said, emphasizing each word.

Lazaro opened his eyes, tilted his head forward, and regarded Diego's dreamy expression with a critical stare. "You didn't know what to do with the seventy-five hundred kilos we were able to get in last year."

"That's not true. I had most of them sold in the first four months."

"And you still haven't figured out where to put the money."

Diego smiled widely. "Also not true." The smile he wore was ironically innocent-looking. Not even Lazaro knew what Diego and Guapo had done to the four diggers, and what Diego had done to Guapo after they dragged the four dead bodies into a wooded area on that chilly January night. "Speaking of which, we need a sub of our own, one reliable enough to make it from South America to California and back."

"Uncle Al already has three in operation and two more under construction. We can use one of those."

"We can, and we will, but I want my own. Get me one of the new ones that are already under construction. I hear those can hold twice as much as the old ones."

Lazaro nodded. "Sixteen thousand kilos and five crew members in the big ones. Takes about six months and four million dollars to build. I'll get on it." He stood and stretched his arms over his head, long heavily-muscled arms with big powerful hands at the ends of them. "I need a few more hours of sleep. Maybe I'll get lucky and dream about Tesla's hot little friend." He chuckled and smiled, picked up the second tumbler of cold water, and headed off to one of the mansion's many bedrooms to get more rest. (There were eight bedrooms and ten bathrooms in the thirty-room mansion.)

Diego got up a moment later and went in search of his lovely lady. He knew where to find her. She was in their second-floor bedroom, probably changing into something less clingy. He could hear the music system blasting her favorite song of the moment: Fantasia's euphonious "Truth Is."

He took the stairs in lieu of the elevator, thinking about the new submarines and all the bricks of Yayo they could hold. *Sixteen thousand kilos of cocaine*, he thought to himself. *I could sell each kilo for fourteen grand and make off with $224 million!*

The numbers excited him to no end. Diego lived for wealth accumulation. Though he believed that reaching Don Pablo's unprecedented level of success in the cocaine business was an impossibility (at the height of Escobar's reign, he had raked in an estimated $100 million a day), Diego was determined to get as close to that level as humanly possible.

At the top of the spiral staircase, his thoughts switched frequencies. Tesla was making a fool of him. He too had overheard her phone conversation in the limo. Dealing with her ex for the sake of their daughter was one thing, but getting involved in her ex's personal life was unacceptable.

He raised his tumbler and finished off his water as he entered the master bedroom, shouldering open the slightly ajar solid mahogany door on the way in. he smelled marijuana smoke in the air, saw it drifting out of the walk-in closet in the east wall. Tesla's dress and heels lay in a heap beside their enormous bed. Diego reached back and pushed the heavy door shut just as Tesla strode out of her closet, wearing nothing at all and smoking a fat blunt, her hair pulled back in a jaunty ponytail.

God, she was stunning.

Diego looked at her fondly. She was close now, less than six feet away, holding the blunt out in front of her, with her Nextel folded shut in the same hand. She was singing along with Fantasia, quite beautifully, really feeling it. Diego wanted badly to cut her off mid-verse and confront her about the phone call, but he couldn't immediately bring himself to do it. Her beauty held him spellbound. Not only her great mane of raven black hair but also those big green eyes, those high cheekbones, her slender nose, her perfectly smooth jawline, her cheeks with their slight dimples, her cherry-brown complexion, those perky young breasts. And those legs … sweet Jesus, those long thick legs of hers were out of this world. He loved the way they tapered so nicely at the ankle yet stayed so voluminous above the knee. They were definitely her second best asset, eclipsed only by her fat round ass.

"Take that shit off," Tesla said as she went to the door and engaged the lock. "You know what time it is. Juicy got me off a triple-stack, this stale-ass blunt I rolled before we left for Vegas got me on one, and that Henny I drank on the jet got my mouth and my pussy wet as fuck. I want you to fuck the shit outta me. None o'that love making shit. Beat it up good."

Diego walked up on her as she was turning to face him. He grabbed her by the throat and shoved her against the door. Her back hit the wood hard. Her eyes got big. She looked up at him' without heels she was only five foot seven, and he was six-two. Several emotions flashed across her gorgeous visage: first shock, then confusion, then a sexually charged grin.

"Keep your communications with Lorenzo to a minimum," Diego said through tightly clenched teeth." If it's not about your daughter, it shouldn't be happening. Comprende?"

"I like it rough." She stuck her tongue out between her teeth, smiled around it.

He tightened his mighty grip on her throat. "You see a smile on my face? I'm not fucking playing with –"

Tesla swung her empty hand up and clutched a handful of his crotch. She squeezed and twisted and pulled all at once, and Diego's grip on her throat loosened very quickly. His hand fell limply away. His eyes bulged out from their sockets. He gasped and winced as an intense, paralyzing pain sent fire lancing throughout his groin area and way up into his gut.

Oddly, though, his cock began to harden in Tesla's fist.

She rose up on her tiptoes and kissed him on the mouth. "I will rip this motherfucker off, Diego. If you ever try me like that again."

"Okay, okay. Just let go," he pleaded.

"I'll never cheat on you, if that's what you're worried about," Tesla said. "But if you think I'm gonna let you dictate who I can and can't talk to on my own goddamn phone, you can find yourself another woman. Because I ain't the one."

She let go of him and he staggered aside, clutching and massaging his aching crotch. His cell phone rang in his pocket. Tesla puffed on her blunt and blew smoke at his face.

She said, "Who is that calling you? Since you wanna monitor my phone calls."

"I bet it's not an ex," he retorted, digging the phone out of his pocket.

Only it was an ex.

Camila Macedo was his ex-girlfriend from West Palm Beach. They'd gotten together in sixth grade and were a couple until their junior year in high school, when Camila's parents relocated to San Diego to be closer to Tijuana, Mexico, their hometown. Diego was beyond surprised to see Camila's mobile phone number on his cell phone screen. They'd kept in touch over the years, and he was always glad to hear from her, but an old schoolmate of theirs had recently informed him of Camila's engagement to an Academy of Art University professor in San Francisco. If that was the case, what was she doing phoning Diego?

"Who you know with a six-one-nine area code?" Tesla asked snappishly.

Diego couldn't help but grin. "My ex Camila," he said, and flipped open the phone. Tesla threw a wild punch at his face. He skillfully parried the blow and stepped around to the opposite side of the bed.

"Hello?" He said into the phone.

The sound of Camila's hysterical sobbing changed Diego's expression from playful to grave. Tesla set her blunt and her phone down on the nightstand and was preparing to crawl across the bed after him when he held up his empty glass and pumped it in the air in a "hold on" gesture.

"What did you do?!" Camila screamed.

"Me?" Diego knitted his brow. "What are you talking about? I haven't done anything."

"They killed him! They killed my fiancé and said it was because of you!"

Chapter 7

Tesla had smoked only about a quarter of her blunt when she put it out, picked up her dress and heels, grabbed her Nextel, and stormed off into her closet. Gazing angrily at her nude reflection in the mirrored sliding doors of her massive closet, she couldn't decide whether she was more upset with Diego for choking her or for trying to control her.

She could hear him now, speaking with his personal attorney, Michael Kazinski, who he'd called immediately after ending the call with his ex-girlfriend. They were trying to put a lid on the story before the news media got a hold of it, to keep Diego's name out of the mix.

Another reason Tesla was pissed at Diego was that she wanted some dead and he wasn't giving it to her. Her nipples were rock-hard and her pussy was super wet, an effect of ecstasy. She'd been hoping to get in a quickie before her mother arrived with Rari. so much for hope.

She put her dress back on and was getting ready to put on her heels when Diego appeared in the doorway. His shirt was unbuttoned, untucked, and open, revealing his well-defined six-pack and pectoral muscles. His black silk tie dangled precariously from the fingers of his veiny right hand. The front of his pants was bulging out.

Tesla's anger evaporated almost instantly.

"Where's that gun I gave you?" Diego asked. He was staring at her ass; she was watching him in the reflection of the mirror.

"It's, um–"

"Stop. you're already in the wrong. Every time I ask you that question, your answer should be 'Right her, cocked and loaded? It's imperative that you keep that gun with you at all times. Even when we're here inside the house."

It took Tesla a long moment to reply. She was practically hypnotized by the bulge in the front of his pants. "Does this, um … have anything to do with whatever happened to your ex?" She asked finally.

Diego swaggered into the closet, his spiffy black dress shoes double-clicking on the gold-veined marble as he walked up behind her and placed his hands on her waist. She felt his hard bulge on her ass. It sent chills up and down her spine, made her inhale deeply and slowly. He put his mouth close to her ear and, in a low whisper, said, "Just obey me, okay? Can you do that?"

Suddenly Tesla felt the need to be submissive, so she nodded her assent. Diego kissed the side of her neck, as if to reward her for her submissiveness. A small voice in the deep recesses of her brain beckoned her to inquire about the incident that had compelled his ex to phone him – she'd heard bits and pieces of it during the conversation between Diego and his lawyer, something about a fiancé being shot and killed in San Francisco – but a louder voice told her to shut up and take off her dress before Diego received another urgent phone call.

Which is what she did. Diego helped her take it off. Then he manipulated his tie into a loop, put it over her head, and made it a makeshift leash. He hurriedly undid his pants and entered her roughly. This would be their first time not using a condom during sex, and Tesla didn't mind one bit.

There were two richly upholstered sofas and four matching armchairs spaced out along one wall. Their luggage – several suitcases and two duffels – stood beside the nearest sofa. Diego had fucked her on that particular sofa eight or nine times, and she half expected him to walk her to it for another round of sofa sex, but he didn't. He bent her over right where she stood, with one hand on her waist and the end of his tie wrapped around the other. His thrusts were fast and furious. She uttered small rhythmic cries, her long ponytail swinging down over her left shoulder like the tassel on a graduation cap. Diego pulled on the tie, and it tightened around her neck. She realized that the choking sensation was turning her on more than anything Diego had ever done to her during intercourse. She watched herself in the reflection of one mirrored sliding door. Asquint and red-veined, her eyes had pupils so largely dilated that the jade green irises surrounding them were hardly visible. The diamonds in her jewelry twinkled in the light. Her breasts bounced wildly about. Diego, an ass man if ever there was one, stared down at her thick jiggling buttocks as he repeatedly rammed his dick against it.

After a while she closed her eyes and began to pant. Her Nextel, clipped to her purse on the sofa, began to ring. Fantasia's "Truth Is", which she'd programmed to repeat once, gave way to Pretty Ricky's "Grind On Me", and halfway through the song Tesla came with a delightful yelp. Her vaginal grip on Diego's dick became a lot more slippery, with his every thrust accompanied by wet, sloshy sounds.

"Si, si, si," Diego said. Yes, yes, yes.

Keyvon had phoned Juicy shortly after she'd left Diego's Stone Mountain estate (which was officially called Casa Grande) in the rear of the stretch Hummer, and they'd agreed to meet up for breakfast at an IHOP they were both known to frequent. The driver let Rhonda out in front of the Buckhead high-rise that housed her ex-boyfriend's upscale condominium, then drove Juicy to the IHOP, helped her pull her suitcase out of the rear storage compartment, and left.

Juicy was not surprised to find her blue Lincoln Navigator sitting in the parking lot. She'd given Keyvon the spare key a few months prior to him moving in with her, and he liked driving it around when she wasn't using it. Ever the gentleman, he got out and hurried over to her, kissed her on the mouth, took her suitcase.

"They found my car somewhere off Gresham," he said. "Whoever had it wrecked it." He started toward the Navigator, wheeling the suitcase behind him. "Ain't nobody seen Lorenzo shit yet."

"What the hell happened?" Juicy asked, walking alongside him.

Keyvon recounted in vivid detail the robbery and carjacking that had occurred as he and Lorenzo were leaving Blaze. As he talked, he loaded Juicy's suitcase into the rear of the Navigator, and she saw that Lorenzo and a pretty girl with extremely short blond-colored hair were looking back at her and Keyvon from the second row seats. They all looked like the robbery had really gotten to them.

"You think it was random?" Juicy asked. "Or do you think somebody set y'all up to get robbed?"

Keyvon shrugged his broad shoulders. "I'll find out soon enough. And when I do …" He didn't finish the sentence. Didn't need to. His reputation for violence was well known throughout the streets of Atlanta. "I got your breakfast on the dash. We already ate."

"Thank you," Juicy said in her absolute sweetest tone. She wanted him to push her against the side of her SUV and kiss her passionately, the way he sometimes did when they were alone. But she knew he'd never show that kind of affection in front of Lorenzo. They were certified street niggas and she was a stripper, and real street niggas didn't kiss strippers. Not in public, at least.

They got in the Navigator, Juicy in the passenger seat, Keyvon behind the wheel. A Styrofoam tray of lukewarm pancakes, sausage, and eggs sat on the dashboard. As Juicy began to eat, the girl in the seat behind Keyvon introduced herself as Debbie. She spoke in an unfamiliar southern drawl.

"Them dirty motherfuckers took my purse," Debbie complained. "I don't even care about the money and jewelry; I can get all that again. It's the other stuff I had in my purse that I really need. My ID, driver's license, social security card, birth certificate. Stuff I need for school, stuff I need for my kids." She let out a guttural groan. "I swear, I hate a broke, bum-ass nigga. Always takin' from their own people."

Lorenzo said, "Juicy, you talked to Tesla?"

Juicy nodded her head, chewing a mouthful of pancake and eggs, watching a globule of maple syrup dangle from a tine on her plastic fork. She swallowed and said, "Have you tried calling her?"

"I just called her twice, and I sent her a text lettin' her know this my new phone number."

Juicy shrugged, picked up her cup of cold orange juice from her cup holder, and drank from the straw. "She might be sleep, Zo. We didn't sleep at all last night, and we were drinkin' on the jet all the way here from Vegas. I'm too tipsy right now. Off a pill, too."

Debbie bent forward in her seat. "Damn, y'all was on a jet? What kinda jet?"

"Girl, a Gulfstream. The G6. And we stayed in a twenty-thousand-dollar-a-night suite at the Bellagio. Rhonda got pulled onstage at this male strip club we went to. We had fun." She turned in her seat to look at Debbie as Keyvon drove out of the parking lot. The girl was beyond beautiful. She had tight blue jeans on her thick legs, small Timberland boots on her feet, a tan-colored turtleneck sweatshirt on her lithe upper body, a diamond stud in her left nostril. Juicy smiled at her. "You know Rhonda. She goes to Spelman with you."

"Rhonda Evergreen?"

"Yep, that's her."

"Oh, she's cool as fuck. We're both studying to be gynecologists. She's heavy into photography too. Smartest girl I've met at Spelman."

Juicy had to force herself to look away from Debbie. Her mind was on some freaky shit. Images of Debbie lying naked in bed flashed in her thoughts and moistened her pussy. She ate in silence for a moment, staring vacantly at her surroundings and listening to a Ciara song that was playing from her speakers, ruminating about Diego's immense wealth and wishing she had just half a percent of it.

"Tesla's boyfriend is a billionaire," she said, after a time. "A twenty-one-year-old billionaire. That bitch hit the lotto, and she ain't even takin' advantage of it."

No one else spoke on the matter, juicy realized that they were all ears, waiting to hear more. At the same time she realized that she had said too much. She was in the presence of three people who'd just been robbed, and here she was bragging about the fun she'd had on some billionaire's private jet. Tesla had strictly forbidden her from mentioning Diego in front of Keyvon and Lorenzo. They'll be jealous of him, Tesla had said, and Zo will take it out on me. He'll start pressing me for money, bringing up old shit, anything to get me to cash him out. Keep them out of my business.

Then a third realization trudged in the front of Juicy's inebriated mind: She *wanted* Lorenzo and Keyvon to be in the know regarding Tesla's relationship with Diego. For one, she was secretly jealous of Tesla and Diego's relationship. Juicy had landed a ghetto millionaire once – Devin "Sleepy" West, a fat black heroin dealer whose network of street dealers in Montgomery, Alabama, brought in a hundred grand a day – but he'd left her for another stripper three months into their relationship. She'd had a two-week fling with Craig "Lil C" Petties, a drug kingpin from the Riverview neighborhood in South Memphis, and their love might have flourished if he hadn't fled to Mexico after a 45-count federal indictment for his arrest was announced. Now Juicy was with Keyvon, a guy who wasn't even her type. The only reason she'd started visiting him when he was incarcerated at Hays Prison was because he was tight with

Enzo and Tesla didn't like going by herself to visit Enzo when he was there. Keyvon was handsome, and he was well built, and his reputation as a real street nigga was known to just about everyone. The only thing that made him not for Juicy was his financial situation. She wanted a baller, a man who could afford to move her into a huge mansion and have her driving around in a Ferrari. She felt like she deserved Diego much more than Tesla did.

Another reason Juicy wanted Lorenzo and Keyvon to know about Diego was that she knew it would piss Lorenzo off. He'd start making demands. Maybe the pressure he'd put on Tesla would compel her to ask Diego for one or two million dollars; Juicy was sure to get a few hundred grand out of that.

"I'm glad for her," Debbie said. "Like I told Zo, Tesla inspired me to be a stripper. I read her story in King magazine last year. She's just like me, you know, a project chick with a sexy face and a fat ass, using what she got to get what she needs, to take care of her kid. I hope she doesn't hate me for being with Zo, because I really do look up to her. Me and the girls at Blaze, we talk about her all the time."

"What's up with that nigga she fuck with?" Lorenzo asked. "What's his name?" Where he from? Why everybody actin' like they can't tell me his name? I need to know what kinda nigga she got my daughter around."

Juicy smiled broadly. 'You gotta ask her, Zo. I can't get in the middle of that. I wasn't even supposed to say what I just said."

"Somebody better tell me somethin'," Zo said, and when Juicy looked over her shoulder at him, he was holding a cell phone to his ear, scowling.

Tesla had lain awake just long enough to hug and kiss her beautiful daughter and listen as Rari described all the fun and not-so-fun things she'd done at her grandmother's apartment over the past five days. Tesla ate two warm toaster pastries and a bowl of cereal while Rari talked. Then Rari ran out of the room with her tongue-bearing pal Diamante yipping at her heels, and Tesla fell into a deep, dreamless sleep. She was awakened once at noon for lunch, and after she ate and used the bathroom she fell into dreamland until 3:30 in the afternoon, when the smells and sounds of soapy bath water being run dragged her from the depths of unconsciousness.

She sat up slowly beneath the twelve-thousand-dollar silk comforter and rested her back on the overstuffed goose-down pillows behind her, blinking away vestiges of dreams. She'd instructed Claire to rouse her at four, so that her first day home with Rari would not be spent sleeping. Now she regrets giving the order. She'd only slept five hours; she felt like she needed five more.

Her mouth was dry. She wanted water, a nice cold drink of it. She wanted to check her cell phone, which she'd left on the sofa in her walk-in closet. She glanced to her left and found everything she needed on the nightstand: a bottle of Fiji water and a twelve-ounce glass full of ice cubes stood on a 24-karat gold serving tray, and between the tray and the shaded Tiffany lamp was her Nextel, powered off to conserve energy, and her purse.

"Thank you so much, Claire," Tesla muttered groggily.

"No trouble, baby," Claire replied from the inside the master bathroom, which was a good thirty feet away.

Tesla filled her glass to the rim and downed a quarter of it while she waited for her Nextel to power on. She found nine missed calls – three from an unknown number; one from her mother; one from her business manager/publicist, Yoshi Lambert; one each from Juicy and Rhonda; and two from the Fulton County jail. There were two new voicemails and seven new text messages. She decided to listen to the voicemails first.

The first one was from Yoshi: "Hey, I just got off the line with Lil Wayne's people. They're shooting a music video in South Beach this coming Wednesday. They want you for a poolside scene in which you're required to wear a skimpy bathing suit. The payday's pretty decent, and the exposure will be good for your career. You'll be one of three booty models standing around him and Birdman, dancing and generally vibing to the music. Oh, and before I forget, Strokers is offering thirty k for you to host Jeezy's mixtape release party tonight. Call me when you get this."

The second voicemail was from Juicy: "Tess, I think you should do whatever you can to help Zo get back on his feet. He really did get robbed. And you know his stupid ass didn't have insurance on that car. He literally lost everything he had. They're sitting in that trap house on Bouldercrest with guns out, about fifteen niggas in the house with em. I made Keyvon come home with me, but he's on the same bullshit. I gave him ten thousand dollars to get right before I left for Vegas. He got robbed for all that. I'm about to smoke me a blunt, get me some dick, and go to sleep. I'll hit you when I get up."

Tesla sighed, shaking her head. She threw back the white silk comforter and swung her legs over the side of the bed. Reluctantly, she stood up and stepped into her white fur Fendi slippers. Grabbed her white silk monogrammed robe off the back of an expensive white fabric chair and put it on to shield her naked body from discourteous eyes. She was bone-tired, and her mind was clouded from all the drinking and drugging she'd done over the past twenty-four hours, but she was cognizant enough to feel some sympathy for Lorenzo's misfortune. He had, after all, given her the most precious gift a man can ever give a woman: a beautiful child. She couldn't abandon him at a time like this. Juicy was right; Tesla had eo do something to help Lorenzo rise back to the top, even if it meant angering Diego again. She couldn't have her baby's father walking around with no money in his pockets, not when she had well over four hundred thousand dollars in her bank account and nearly the same amount of cash right here in the mansion.

The sound of rushing water stopped. Claire walked out of the bathroom and gave Tesla a warm, matriarchal smile. "Your bath water's ready. Dotty just got Rari to take a nap. She's curled up in bed with that damned dog."

Tesla managed a sleepy grin. "You and that dog."

"I hate it."

"Diego didn't leave, did he?"

"He did. He left out with Laz after they ate lunch. Said something about a flight to San Diego. Don't quote me. I'm not sure if he was taking a flight there or if he had someone flying in."

"Did Pari leave with him?"

"Yes."

"Then he was the one on that flight," Tesla said bitterly.

"She prepared dinner before they left out," Claire said, planting her fists on her hips. "Her and the two assistant cooks. They whipped up some pan-seared duck breast beef tartare, rillettes, gumbo shrimp – you know, the usual rich people stuff."

"I'll be down in thirty."

Tesla was suddenly wide awake. Judging from the tense conversation she'd overheard between Diego and his lawyer, Diego's ex-girlfriend Camila lived in San Diego. What in god's name was Diego doing flying off to see his ex? She'd been grabbed by the throat for the simple offense of discussing what had happened to her ex with her own mother. Now Diego was going to visit his ex? On the first day of him and Tesla being back in each other's presence since last week?

She was a mile past pissed.

In the bathtub, Tesla lay back in the sudsy tepid water, flicked open her cell phone, and began reading her text messages. There was one from Rhonda: *Just made it home, forcing myself to sleep now.* The mother of Tesla's brother Marlon's daughter had sent two messages telling Tesla to answer the collect call from Marlon, and two of his side chicks had sent similar messages. Tesla was just about to check the next message when her phone rang. It was the unfamiliar number.

"Hello? She answered.

"Damn, you can't answer the muhfuckin phone? For me?" Lorenzo's voice brimmed with indignation. "You turned your phone off?"

"No, I didn't. Claire turned it off to keep the battery from draining. She always does that. I was sleeping. And before you start going in on me about me not helping you out, stop and listen to what I have to say." She paused, studying her fingernails and cuticles. "I got about fifty thousand for you. If you can't get right with that, I don't know what to tell you. Buy yourself a brand-new Mercedes. No more old schools. Lease a new Mercedes and I'll help you make the payments if need be. *Get insurance.* Okay? No excuses. Fall back from the streets for a few weeks, get your mind right. And if I hear you spent my money on that new ho you got, we gon' have problems."

Lorenzo was silent for a moment. When he spoke again, Tesla could almost hear the burgeoning joy in his winsome voice.

"I knew you still loved me," he said.

"Oh, shut up."

"So you don't love me no more?"

"I *abhor* you."

"You what?"

"Abhor. Loathe. Hate." Tesla had learned the first two words from Rhonda, but she wasn't about to tell Lorenzo that. "Have you heard anything about your car?"

"It's some niggas from around here. Gotta be. They found kilo's car a few blocks from here. Word on the street is it was some niggas who run wit' Red , that Zone Six Clique, mad 'cause was over her trappin' on Bouldercrest."

"You should've just stayed in Bankhead, Zo. Then you wouldn't be havin' these problems."

"When you comin' through with that money?"

"Well, I'm in the tub now, and Rari just –"

"You in the bathtub? Naked?"

Tesla rolled her eyes and smiled. "Naaaaah, I'm fully clothed," she said, sarcasm dripping off her every word.

"I can't believe you ain't gave me no pussy since I been out. What kinda shit is that? I used to tear dat pussy up."

"Don't get hung up on, Lorenzo," Tesla said, but she didn't really mean it. If there was one thing she'd enjoyed during her intimate relationship with Lorenzo it was the sex. His dick was huge, and he had extraordinary stamina. He didn't eat pussy – that was a depressing fact – but he'd more than made up for it in other ways.

"Okay, okay, my bad. You're right," he said.

"I know I'm right. I'm always right."

"Call or text me when –"

"No, you get to my mom's new house and wait for me there. Get out of that trap house. If you're not at that house helping her move in when I get there, you can kiss that fifty grand good-bye."

She flipped the phone shut abruptly, placed it on the ledge of the tub, and sank deeper into the soapy warm water. Her thoughts wandered to Diego and the bitch who'd phone him from San Diego. Now that her mind was clearer, Tesla could think with a reasonable amount of intelligence. The first thought that came to mind was a question: Was Diego cheating on her with his ex?

"Two can play that game," Tesla said aloud, sneering at her immaculately pedicured toenails.

Then came another disconcerting question: Was someone plotting to come after her in the same way they'd gone after Diego's ex-girlfriend's fiancé? If there was any correlation between that murder and the ominous warning Diego had given her in Las Vegas, she needed to take action. She was beginning to think Rhonda's suspicions of the Santos family were spot-on. Maybe they really were tied to some kind of

Colombian drug cartel. Maybe the cornerstone of the Santos family's tremendous wealth and power was the clandestine world of organized crime.

Tesla pondered these possibilities as she soaked and bathed. The more she ruminated about the possible threats, the more she became convinced that they were very real. She believed that she and her daughter were safe here at the Casa Grande estate, but she wasn't confident that Big Rick alone could keep her out of harm's way if she were to be confronted by a gunman in public.

She stood up and stepped out of the bathtub. Drying herself with a five-hundred-dollar monogrammed Pratesi bath towel, she said, "okay, Tesla – think. Assume your boyfriend is involved with a drug cartel. What could that do to better your situation?"

She answered her own question: "I could act as an intermediary between Diego's people and my people. Yeah." She smiled at the bright idea as she scooped up her cell phone, put on her silk robe and slippers, and left the bathroom for her walk-in closet. "I could help turn my brother and my baby's daddy into kingpins. That way if Diego ever leaves me, I'll still have access to Marlon and Lorenzo's money." She nodded her head. "Yes. Definitely. Si, si, si."

Chapter 8

Tesla got dressed. Black-lace Victoria's Secret bra and thong panties set. Tight black leather pants, black turtleneck sweatshirt, black leather bomber jacket, black leather sneakers – all Gucci. She put on a heresy Cartier watch, dumped everything from the purse she'd used yesterday into a black croc skin Hermes Birkin bag, and then slid a thirteen-shot magazine into the gold-plated Glock and very carefully pulled back the slide. She pushed the gun and extra mags down into the Birkin, added a fat pair of diamond-encrusted hoop earrings to her lobes and a simple thirty-thousand-dollar white diamond necklace to her neck, and picked up her phone to chirp Big Rick, who lived nearby in a less costly section of Stone Mountain. Then thinking of his pregnant wife, she changed her mind and clipped the Nextel to the waistline of her pants.

"Let him spend some quality time with his wife," Tesla muttered as she rifled through her Louis Vuitton suitcase for the cash she'd brought with her from Las Vegas. "Diego's paying him anyway. For all I know he could be Diego's eyes and ears."

She found the cash right where she'd left it, put it all in her Birkin bag, and began putting away her things from the suitcases. She was just finishing up when Rari and the dog traipsed into the closet, Rari looking sleepy, Diamante looking like someone had laced his doggie treats with cocaine. Dotty, the Jamaican nanny who looked after Rari, was seconds behind them. Tesla sent Dotty to grab one of Rari's coats.

"Ma," Rari said, climbing onto the sofa in her hot-pink Barbie sundress and floral-print leggings, "Can we please go see my real daddy today? And my sisters? I wanna see my sisters too." She sounded just as sleepy as she looked.

"We're about to go and see him. You'll see Aliyah and Jasmine this Wednesday. What do you want for dinner?"

"Ice cream. Cookie dough ice cream."

"Besides ice cream."

Rari yawned, arching her back and rubbing her eyes with the sides of her forefingers. Her hair – long and silky straight like Tesla's – was braided into plaits with pink beads at the ends. Three carat diamond studs glistened in her earlobes. "Pizza," she said finally. "Pizza for dinner, ice cream for dessert." Her mouth spread open in an exuberant, toothy smile. Tesla's smile.

Tesla rolled her eyes and shook her head. You little brat, she thought, putting on her diamond rings. "I don't know, Rari. The chefs already prepared dinner. Pan-seared duck breast."

Rari grimaces in disgust. "I'd rather eat dog poop. Yuck."

"You are so dramatic."

"Who thought it was a good idea to eat a duck? That's nasty. Grandma don't cook no ducks. She only cooks chickens. I like chicken." She slipped down off the sofa, her pink-and-white Nikes missing Diamante's hind leg by mere centimeters as she landed. "Ma, can I ask you something?" She gave no room for a reply. "How come my daddy can't stay here with us? This house is so big. It's like a million of Grandma's apartments all put together."

Tesla was thinking of a gentle way to answer Rari when her cell phone rang on her hop. Walking out of the closet, with Rari and Diamante trailing close behind her, she answered the call. It was Yoshi. Tesla confirmed both the mixtape release party hosting gig and the Miami Beach video shoot, a combined payday of $40,000, ten percent of which would go to Yoshi. While Dotty helped Rari into a hot pink Barbie coat, Tesla and Yoshi discussed several other modeling gigs, including a photo shoot for smooth magazine and seven more club appearances in four different states.

"You could be making a lot more if you returned to the pole," Yoshi said. "There's a strip club in Baltimore that's willing to pay you fifty-k to hit the stage. They know that you're the talk of the industry right now, and having your face on a flyer will boost the popularity of their nightclubs. You could do a cross country strip club tour and charge fifty grand every time you hit the stage. Book twenty of those, that's a million dollars on top of what you'll make while you're dancing. You're missing out on a lot of money, Tesla. This opportunity comes once in a lifetime."

"Yeah, I know, but my man doesn't want me stripping."

"Unless he's some kinda multimillionaire who just put a ring on your finger, I'd suggest you start working on securing your own future. You're my second-most famous client, yet you're bringing in less than my *least* famous client. This is your moment. Do you not understand that? Get yourself a few million in the bank while you got the chance. Fame doesn't last all that long. Take advantage while you still have it."

"Can we talk about this later?"

"If you keep procrastinating there won't be a later. I'll see you at Strokers. Nine o'clock. Don't be late."

"I won't."

Tesla folded her cell phone shut. She saw that Rari was still looking up at her, waiting on a response, but Tesla's mind was elsewhere. She was contemplating the strip club tour, and wondering where the hell Diego had flown off to. Yoshi had been pressuring Tesla to start stripping again since before Thanksgiving last year, but Tesla had always held off out of respect for Diego. Now she was having second thoughts. Diego was making money hand over fist, while

Tesla's income had essentially become stagnant. Sure, he had given her over six hundred thousand dollars, and the pink slips to her two vehicles were in her name, but that didn't take away from the fact that she wasn't making the kind of money she used to make.

And there was something else that had Tesla wanting to take a more serious stance towards her own financial independence. The phone call Diego had gotten from his ex had Tesla feeling deeply insecure. She'd lost men to other women in the past. Lorenzo had cheated on her numerous times. Two other boyfriends had left her after she'd refused to stop stripping, and another boyfriend had left her for another exotic dancer.

Was she about to lose Diego to his ex-girlfriend?Clenching her teeth as she preceded Dotty and Rari out of the bedroom, Tesla flipped open her cell phone and dialed Diego's number.

Contrary to what Tesla believed, Diego had not flown via private jet to be close to his high school sweetheart in California; he'd flown his high school sweetheart via private jet to be close to him in Georgia.

Camila Macedo had sustained a minor graze wound to the nape of her neck in the assault on her husband-to-be, which had taken place as he backed his SUV out of their driveway. A gunmen on a black motorcycle had rolled to a stop alongside the SUV and fired directly into the driver's window, hitting Frank Ortiz three times in the head. Camila had thrown open the passenger's door and jumped out as the armed motorcyclist sped away.

"We were going to the gym," she'd said to Diego as they left the Atlanta airport in the back seat of his triple-black Phantom. "I've been exercising a lot, so I can look good in my wedding gown. Frank wanted to shed twenty pounds before our June nuptials. This wasn't supposed to happen.

We weren't involved i anything illegal. Frank is the kindest man I've ever met."

"They said my name?"

"Yes. 'Blame Diego,' and then he started shooting."

"And you didn't tell that to the detectives?"

"No. I only told them about the shooting, and that the guy had the letters M-A-R-A tattooed on his fingers. I couldn't see his face because of the helmet, but I heard him clearly. He definitely said, 'Blame Diego'."

Diego had booked Camila into a five-thousand-dollar-a-night suite at the Marriott Marquis on Peachtree Center Avenue. He'd wired money to her mother, a retired Mexican school teacher, so that her parents could come and be with her in Atlanta. He'd walked her into the hotel, trying his best to keep his eyes off her curvaceous figure. He'd accompanied her into the suite and held her while she cried on his shoulder. He'd given her an envelope with ten thousand dollars in it and promised to get to the bottom of her fiancé's murder. He'd waited with her until the security detail he had hired over the phone arrived – four large men with huge muscles and holstered guns on their waists – and then he'd left, promising to return by nightfall.

Now, as he regarded the bound and bloodied Salvadoran man duct-taped to the wooden armchair across from him with a frigid stare, he couldn't get the image of Camila's distraught, puffy-eyed face out of his head. The image infuriated him.

Which explained why he was sitting here in Alejandro Ramero's kitchen with Lazaro and ten Colombian sicarios (goon) standing around him. It was a nice-sized home, a few thousand square feet of living space, each room clean and well-furnished; a two-car garage with two BMW 745 sedans parked in it. Diego estimated its worth as being somewhere in the neighborhood of six hundred grand, and he assumed the corpulent woman who was now hog-tied between two small children in the living room was ultimately responsible for its tidiness.

Alejandro's right eye was swollen and completely shut. There were knots and ugly lacerations all over his face. His long dark hair was matted with blood. He had on a pair of white shorts that were now dotted with blood. No t-shirt, no shoes; Lazaro had his entire chest, abdomen, and lower legs, and there were more tats on his neck and arms. They were gang-related tattoos. Alejandro Romero was a high-ranking MS-13 gang member.

"Somebody in your organization made an enormous mistake this morning," Diego said. He was sitting in an identical chair, facing Alejandro, wearing a navy Tom Ford suit and tie with a pocket square and diamond cufflinks. His phone began to ring in his pocket, but for the moment he ignored it. "You can help yourself out here, Alejandro. Do you want to do that?"

Alejandro said nothing.

Diego's phone went on ringing.

"This can end one of two ways, Alejandro. Either you live or you die. If you die" – Diego turned his head and looked toward the living room – "They die."

"What do you want from me? Eh? Eh?"

"Tell me who ordered the shooting in San Francisco this morning."

"How would I know? I'm in Atlanta, been here eight years." Blood trickled down his chin and spotted his shorts. "Look, if you want money, I'll give you money. There's sixty-five grand in a backpack in my bedroom closet, another fifty in the big red toolbox in my garage. Take it and leave and I'll forget your faces."

"Who authorizes the hits in California?"

Alejandro scowled at Diego with his one good eye. "What are you, a Fed?"

"Feds don't duct-tape and abuse their suspects. Who authorized the hit?"

Alejandro said nothing.

"Somebody grab his wife," Diego said, standing up. "Cut off her fingers one by one until this idiot starts talking. I have to take this call."

"Wait," Alejandro said, actually it was more of a growl. "Is that all you fucking want? A fucking name?"

"No. What I want is a name, an address, and a phone number." Diego had his Nextel out and was staring at Tesla's number at the top of his missed calls log. "I have things to do, Mr. Romero. I'm a busy man. An *important* man, in the grand scheme of it all. How do you think I got your address? How do you think I found out that you and your MS-13 crew have been moving kilos for the Beltran Leyva cartel for approximately nineteen months, and that you used some of the proceeds to finance the purchase of this quaint little home of yours? I'm somebody, Alejandro, the polar opposite of what you are. The only way you're getting out of this alive is if you tell me what I need to know."

"How do I know you won't kill me after you get what you need?"

"I'm a man of my word, Alejandro. Anyone who knows me will tell you that. If you help me get to the bottom of this, not only will I let you and your family survive this … unfortunate intrusion. I'll also connect you with the guys who supply the Beltran Leyva cartel. You'll be making double what you're making now, maybe even triple. Within five or six months you'll be making a hundred times more than you're making now."

The look in Alejandro's unswollen eye became less angry and more inquisitive. He opened his mouth to speak, then closed it, then opened it again and said, "What are you, some kinda Mexican kingpin?"

"No, sir, Mr. Romero. I'm Colombian. I'm a kingpin maker."

93

The digital clock on Juicy's night table read 5:07 pm when she woke to the sound of excited voices, the voices of men. It sounded like they were in her living room. One of the voices belonged to Keyvon. Another belonged to Ralph, Keyvon's half-brother from Macon, Georgia. The other was unfamiliar.

Juicy's home was a modest two-story vinyl-sider that was thirty years old and would take at least that long to pay off. Located on Glenn Street, the house stood right in the middle of Zone 3, in a predominantly black section where drug-dealing and prostitution were commonplace and crime was rife. The house had three bedrooms, which gave Juicy's ten-year-old twins, Tashaco and Michael Brand Jr., their own bedrooms. Juicy's paternal aunt Christina, the woman who'd raised her, lived in the basement with 19-year-old boyfriend. Juicy had left Christina in charge of the household while she was gone. Soon, she knew Aunt Christina would be paying her a bedroom visit to collect babysitting fees.

A perpetual eavesdropper, Juicy slipped out of bed in her small t-shirt and smaller boy shorts and tiptoed to the bedroom door to get a closer listen on Keyvon's conversation. She'd been trying to catch him cheating for the longest, or at least to catch him admitting to cheating. Then she could kick him to the curb and start dating a bigger baller without feeling too bad about it.

The door was open a few degrees. She put her ear to the crack and listened.

"My nigga Guay wanna buy the cutty as-is, say he got fifty for it," Ralph was saying. "He got a nigga who can switch out the VIN numbers."

Keyvon said, "Yeah, tell him to come on with that. Bring the money ever here. Did y'all get that garbage bag out the trunk?"

"Yep. it was full of one-dollar bills. I used that to pay JT for lettin' us use his Suburban. He got a lil over three thousand."

"A'ght. So it's just me, you, and this ugly muhfucka. All this money right here came outta my pocket. We can split the fifty racks between us three." Keyvon paused; Then "Wait, it was four of y'all. Who was the fourth one?"

"His dike-ass sister. You thought it was a man, didn't you?" Ralph laughed.

"Fuck you," the third man said.

"Y'all plan on paying her?" Keyvon asked.

"She kept the purse," said the third man. "I guess it was worth a few racks , and it had like twelve hundred in it."

Eyes and mouth agape, Juicy tiptoed back to her bed and sat down. She couldn't believe her ears. Keyvon had not been a victim in last night's armed robbery and carjacking. He'd been in on it.

"I used to dance too, you know, "Claudia said to Debbie as they sat in her year-old Mercedes-Benz G-Wagon with the windows up, passing a blunt of dro back and forth while the boys – Claudia's boyfriend Donny and two of his nephews; Lorenzo and his cousin Bo –carried the last few boxes into the house. "At Club Gold on Piedmont. I was dancing there when I met the father of my kids. Walter Harrison. He was a heroin dealer, used to pull up to the strip club in that clean-ass '76 El Dorado. I was only sixteen when I started stripping, and Walt got me pregnant the first time we fucked. I worked the pole for almost fourteen years on and off, then I gave up when Walt got killed. Been working nine-to-five ever since. Took me forever to find a job that didn't piss test me."

"Tesla looks so much like you." Debbie toked on the blunt and coughed. Like Claudia, she had her seat fully reclined. She passed the blunt back to Claudia. "I swear, you and her can almost pass for twins.

"If I had a nickel for every time I heard that. You should see Nikola, my oldest daughter. She's twenty-one, looks even more like me in the face than Tesla does."

"Can you give me any advice on how to get to where Tesla is? Financially I mean."

"I'll tell you like I told her," Claudia said. "Be all about your money. If some rich lawyer offers you five thousand dollars to stomp on his balls and piss in his mouth, get that money. And most importantly, save your money. Open yourself a savings account. Put a hundred dollars in it every week and don't take nothing out of it for five or six years. Don't blow all your money on expensive cars and designer handbags, because that shit will have you broke in a year's time. Don't ever use anything stronger than weed, because that shit will have you broke in a week. Take advantage of the opportunity you have to network with all the folks you see in the club. Exchange phone numbers, get to know them no matter how broke they might look because they just might be the next to blow. I love Lorenzo like a son, I really do, but don't let your love for him fuck up your future. If you catch you a millionaire, or a nigga you know is about to be a millionaire, leave Lorenzo's ass right where you found him. Forget about love. It's all about the money, baby. You with me so far?"

Debbie nodded her head emphatically.

"If he really loves you, he'll take you back later on down the line," Claudia went on. "He'll understand. Shit, he might even benefit from it. One of the girls I danced with at Club Gold married a wealthy stock broker, divorced his ignorant ass three years later, and ended up with ten million dollars and two mansions when it was all said and done. She moved that same street nigga she was with before she got married into the same house she stayed in with her husband, and they been together ever since. You need to think like her, you hear me?"

Debbie nodded again.

"Marry into some money if you can't get rich on your own. Your first marriage should always be for the money. Don't ever forget that. Tesla had just started messing around with Porky from Edgewood when she met Diego. Porky had long money, heroin money, but it was street money. Street money don't last that long. Diego had that legit money. Real estate money. So you know what I told her? I said, "You need to leave Porky right where you found him and get serious with Dee.' And she did it. Now look at her. She's living the high life. My baby got bodyguards and maids, chefs and personal trainers, her own team of hair and makeup people. Her car alone is worth two hundred and eighty grand. And it's hers, you know. That's another thing. If a man ever offers to buy you a car, tell him you don't want it unless your name is on that pink slip as the owner. That way he'll never be able to take it back. This G-Wagon was bought by that football player she was seeing early last year. She gave it to me when Dee bought her that Range Rover, signed it right over to me. That's how boss bitches move."

Debbie nodded slowly and thoughtfully. "What about getting into music videos? Can you give me any game on that? Because I've met a lot of people in the music biz, both in Houston and her in Atlanta, but all I keep getting is the runaround. Empty promise after promise."

"You need to get your phone number into the hands of the artists, but most importantly you need to get you phone number into the hands of the producers. Video producers. Check out your favorite music videos, find out who produced them, and contact them by phone or email. They're the ones who matter. A nigga will sell you a million and one dreams in the strip club." Claudia sat up, coughing harshly and staring at the dro-filled Swisher pinched between her manicured thumb and forefinger as if she had just now realized the marijuana's potency. "I'm putting this out," she said.

"Please do. I'm about to die in here."

Claudia extinguished the blunt and lowered the windows to let the SUV air out. The temperature outside was a lot warmer than it had been earlier in the day. She sucked in a breath of fresh spring air and studied her bloodshot green eyes in the visor mirror. She looked remarkably young for thirty-seven. Named after her father's beloved mother, she was 100% Cuban. Her long black hair went way down to her lower back when it wasn't wrapped up in a headscarf as it was now. It was a Fendi head scarf that she had borrowed from Tesla and never returned. Of the three 18-karat gold Herringbone necklaces she wore, only one of them had a pendant, a gold cross with real white diamonds embedded in it. She kept her smooth reddish brown skin moisturized, her full lips glossed, her lashes darkened with mascara. She had her old stripper name, Cubana Doll, inked into the left side of her neck in cursive lettering. She was five foot six, an inch shorter than Tesla, and she was just as thick in the derriere. She had on a smug white Gucci t-shirt over tight black sweatpants and Michael Jordan sneakers, as the temperature had risen from forty-eight degrees this morning to an even seventy now.

She looked over at Debbie, a short pretty girl with a short ugly car. Debbie's dark red Ford Escort was parked across the street. She seemed much too put together to be pushing a hoopty. Her purse and the belt looped around the waist of her Apple Bottom jeans were also Louis. Her Nike Air Max sneaks looked brand-new. Her red t-shirt ended midriff; it showed off her trim waistline and the small diamond in her navel.

"You must've just started dancing," Claudia said.

"I did. It'll be three weeks tomorrow. I have two kids back home in Houston. My whole family is in the hood. McDonald's wasn't cutting it, and I'm too scared of jail to be selling drugs. I had to do something."

"How much are you making at Blaze?"

"About a thousand dollars a night. I made that in a month at Mickey D's. Last night I walked out with over *three thousand*. It was all in the trunk of Lorenzo's car when we got robbed. I had another twelve hundred in my purse, which they also took."

"You got any money in the bank?"

"Yeah. it's not much, though. I just paid for my mama and my kids to move out of my granny's apartment and into their own place. I had to get all my books and supplies for school, now outfits to dance in, regular clothes to wear, food, makeup, and toiletries. I'm living with my cousin Quincy. He had a one-bedroom apartment but the building owner let him upgrade to a two-bedroom so I could move in. I had to get a five-piece bedroom set, a TV and DVD player, cable, new carpeting, and all the other stuff I needed for the bedroom. Plus I agreed to split the rent and utilities with him. It seems like all my money is gone before I even get it. I only got like four grand in my bank account."

"Trade in that car and get yourself something nice. You need to look presentable."

"I know. That damned putt-putt keeps breaking down on me. I don't like driving it. My girl, Shanita's aunt, works at a luxury car dealership in Buckhead. She helped Shanita get a brand-new S550 for only eight grand down and seven hundred a month and Shanita's credit score is lower than mine. Basically all you gotta do is come to her with ten percent of what the car costs and be prepared to make the monthly payments. I'm thinking about getting me a Benz too."

"Hurry up and do that." Claudia was lighting a Newport. "You don't want people looking at you like you need them. You gotta look like money. Don't spend all your money trying to look good, but you definitely have to invest in yourself?" She puffed on her cigarette, thinking of more advice to give. "Do you dance every night?"

"Pretty much. I take afternoon classes at Spelman, dance at night, and sleep in the mornings."

"Start spreading yourself around to other strip clubs. Hit up Jazzy T's, Magic City, Strokers. You'll make more money that way. The guys will be more excited to see you when you make an appearance, and they'll spend more to get your attention. Plus it'll get you more exposure. That's how Tesla got her name out there."

"Really?"

"Really." Claudia blew a stream of tobacco smoke out her window. After smoking the blunt, the cigarette tastes like a small slice of heaven. "It's how she was able to buy this house. She paid cash for it, you know. A hundred and eighty-five thousand dollars, plus another hundred and twenty thousand in renovations. I think Dee paid for some of the renovations, but Tesla paid for the house. I made her save a week's pay every month. No exceptions. Twenty-five percent of her monthly income went into her savings account.

"I'm about to start doing that," Debbie said, smiling excitedly and buzzing her seat to an upright position. She was clearly enthused about what she was learning. "Can I get your phone number so I can call you for advice when I need it? I promise not to bug you too much. I'll even pay you."

"Baby, you ain't gotta pay me no money. Pay me by succeeding. Pay me by paying it forward to the next young black woman in need of some good advice. You got a pen?"

Debbie did have a pen. She dug it out of her purse and was jotting down Claudia's mobile phone number when Claudia heard the distinctive growl of her youngest daughter's Ferrari F430 coupe rounding the corner onto Church Street.

Tesla had overdressed. She'd sent Dotty back into the mansion with her and Rari's coats as soon as she stepped out into the heat, and now, as she pulled to the curb behind her mother's matte black G-Wagon, she peeled off her sweatshirt.

"It's too hot for all this, Ma. Ain't it?" Rari asked, looking up at Tesla from her booster seat, her big precious green eyes searching for validation in the face of her all-knowing mommy.

"It definitely is," Tesla said. She unbuckled her seatbelt and pointed at the tall dark-skinned man who was exiting the wrought-iron gate at the start of the walkway that led to her mother's front porch. "You see him? Who is that?"

Rari looked and gasped. Her eyes got big. Her mouth fell open. "Daddy!" She began fumbling with her seatbelt, eliciting an ingratiating grim from Tesla.

Lorenzo opened Rari's door, undid her seatbelt, and plucked her out of the booster seat, planting kisses on the side of her laughing face as he perched her on his muscular black forearm. He had on a white wife beater that was smudged with dirt in places, buggy red sweatpants.

Tesla pushed open her door, shouldered her purse, and rose out just as Dotty steered her Range Rover around the corner. There were no more parking spaces in front of Claudia's house, and the moving truck was in Claudia's gated driveway, so Dotty used a neighbor's driveway to turn around and parked behind a beat-up red Ford Escort across the street.

Tesla took a moment to look around before she joined Lorenzo and Rari on the sidewalk. A blue jay zipped across in front of her, narrowly dodging a passing car before soaring upward, catching a warm breeze, and gliding away. She glanced into the car. Husband and wife in the front, and a kid in the back in a booster seat. Another one next to him, older. Maybe eight. The rear bumper had a sticker. It read: *MY KID IS AN HONOR ROLL STUDENT AT CEDAR GROVE ELEMENTARY.*

Three young black men stood around a clean gray Dodge Magnum three car lengths behind her Ferrari. One was older, bigger, the alpha male. The others were sidekicks, only there for laughs and to send on errands. Then Tesla noted the five young black children playing with Nerf guns in a neighboring yard while three young black women in casual springtime attire sat talking on the porch steps.

On the other neighboring porch, two old black men. In their late seventies, at least. Sitting in fold out chairs and drinking cold bottles of Budweiser, convivial old beer buddies enjoying their golden years. In the alleyway behind Claudia's impressive new home, a motley assortment of black teenagers walked and talked, one of them holding a stocky brown pit-bull on a chain.

Across the street a man stood leaning against a champagne-colored Jaguar sedan, jabbering away on his cell phone. Girbaud t-shirt, matching denim shorts, fresh white low-top Air Force Ones. sparkling rose gold Rolex on his right wrist. He was too short and the wrong build for a pro athlete. Dressed far too nicely for a low level drug-dealer. Tesla figured he was an upper echelon dope boy, with two or three kilos to his name and a crew of young dealers under his control.

All eyes fell on Tesla as she sauntered around the front of her Ferrari and onto the sidewalk. She noted that overt stares but paid them no mind. Her eyes were on Lorenzo Hollis. She'd only seen him once since his release from Hays, when he and Keyvon stopped by Claudia's apartment the day he got out. He had sat down with Rari on his knee and explained in great detail how his then girlfriend Monika had swindled him out of all his cash and belongings. Tesla had gone right into her purse and given him a ten-thousand dollar packet of hundreds. She hadn't hugged him that day out of respect for Diego, but she had wanted to.

She had wanted to do a helluva lot more than hug him.

"So this the car I keep hearing about," he said, studying the F430's sleek exterior, his winsome smile displaying his solid gold champers. "This yours?"

Tesla nodded, suppressing a smile of her own. "We need to talk," she said.

"We definitely need to talk," he said, and now his eyes were on Tesla, smoldering brown eyes that had once made her melt at will. During his stint in prison, she had taken Rari to visit him once a month, sometimes twice a month, and she had noted his burgeoning muscles every visit. His body was ridiculous. Rock-hard abs, massive biceps and triceps, brawny shoulders and pecs. He looked Tesla up and down, bit the corner of his bottom lip, and nodded his approval. In a low voice, he said, "You lucky my girl right there."

"Right where?" Tesla asked, a little too quickly.

He tilted his head toward Claudia's G-Wagon just as the driver's and passenger's doors swung open. A diminutive redbone with low-cut blond-colored hair – hardly any hair at all, really – and a fat bubble butt hopped down from the passenger's seat. She was a bad bitch; Tesla couldn't deny it, not even to herself.

Claudia came around from the driver's side of the G-Wagon and stepped up onto the curb. "Come on inside, y'all. I ain't unpacked yet, but we got all the furniture in order. We can sit down."

The short girl smiled at Tesla and gave a finger-fluttering wave. Reluctantly, Tesla reciprocates the gesture. A small part of her reluctance was induced by jealousy, but most of it was because she was instinctively cautious of strangers. Especially strangers with access to her daughter.

They headed into the front yard, with Dotty taking up the rear. She was a slender 26-year-old with dark skin, braided locs, a bunch of ear piercings, and an innate proclivity for chain smoking cigarettes. She was of average size and height, an outright dullard despite having obtained a bachelor's degree in child psychology from a local community college, semi-attractive. The oversized tote bag Tesla had bought her to carry Rari's things in was strapped to her shoulder.

Looking up as they neared the enclosed sunporch, Tesla counted one rotating camera above the door and three more just under the roof.

"Ten goddamn cameras on this house," Claudia said, climbing the steps. "Four more in the garage. One in the garage. Feel like I'm in a damn James Bond movie."

"Won't nobody be sneaking up on you," Tesla reasoned. She wondered what Mama would say if she learned that the walls were insulated with an expensive bullet-resistant foam, and that the doors and windows were bulletproof.

"Let a nigga try to sneak up on me if he want to," Claudia said feistily. "I got a big ole pistol. Bet I'll be the last bitch he sneaks up on."

Dotty said, "I smell the ganja. Somebody smoked something strong."

Tesla smelled it too, a powerful marijuana odor that made her mouth water. It was wafting off either Claudia or the short pretty girl, or maybe off both of them.

They stepped into the living room. It was elegantly furnished in brown leather and steel with a polished hardwood floor and a 65-inch Sony television with a DVD player on top of it. Incredibles, two-year-old Marlana's favorite movie, was playing on the screen, while Marlana herself snoozed under a Minnie Mouse blanket on the love seat. Lamps and ashtrays and framed photographs decorated the end tables.

"This is by far the nicest house I've ever moved into," Claudia said. She plopped down at the far end of the sofa. "Everything is so new and fresh. All this leather, all that stainless steel in the kitchen, the marble floors in the kitchen and basement. I'm glad I drove over here and looked around before we got the U-Haul. You didn't tell me the whole damn house was already furnished. Now I gotta get rid of that old furniture."

"Just make sure my baby keeps her own room," Tesla said, "And remember that those three bedrooms upstairs are for me, Marlan, and Nikola. Don't let me find out you let somebody lay their funky asses in our beds. I bought this house for us."

Claudia puffed on her cigarette, sighed dramatically, and rolled her eyes.

There were two bedrooms on the first floor. The door in the west wall of the living room opened into Rari's princess-themed bedroom. The door in the south wall of the living room opened into Claudia's master bedroom. Tesla had personally selected the furnishings. In Claudia's bedroom, everything from the sheets and pillowcases to the rugs and curtains were Versace. The Sam decor existed in Tesla's upstairs bedroom, only her color scheme was white, whereas Claudia's was black.

"Let's not forget who the mam is," Claudia said, tapping a roll of ash off her cigarette. "Rari, go on in there and check out your room. I'm sure it ain't nothing like your room at Diego's place, but it's yours."

An inherently grateful child, Rari was all smiles as Lorenzo put her down so she could go in and investigate her new home away from home. "Thank you!" She yelled as she sprinted into her bedroom, followed seconds later by Dotty.

"Marlon got his own place anyway," Claudia went on. "Oh, and he called me twice today looking for you and Zo, said it was important. Bastard wouldn't tell me what it was about. He should be calling back when they let him out his cell again."

Tesla nodded her head. She and Lorenzo were standing beside the coffee table. Being in such close proximity to the man she'd been so madly in love with just a few years prior was overwhelming. She didn't like the fact that his girlfriend was at his other side.

"Hi," the girl said, giving another peculiar wave. "I'm Debbie. I'm a big fan of yours."

Tesla forced a smile. "Aww, thanks." She turned to Lorenzo. "Let's talk in my mama's room. You too, Debbie. I wanna hear all about this robbery." She actually wanted to speak with Lorenzo in private, but it didn't seem appropriate.

As the three of them strode into Claudia's bedroom, Donny shouted from somewhere in the rear of the house that he was getting ready to return the U-Haul truck and stop by the liquor store. His nephews, Daquan and Deric, were riding with him, and he needed Claudia to trail them in her SUV and give them a ride back.

"I'll be here until you get back," Tesla said to Claudia.

"We won't be long." Claudia stepped into the bedroom doorway. "You bring any cash with you? I just went grocery shopping yesterday; spent the last money I had in my purse."

Tesla rolled her eyes. "Ain't no need to lie, Ma. I brought you some money."

"Who's lying?" Claudia grinned guilty. "Let's not forget that I'm helping your sister with her bills, I'm helping your aunt Thelma with her bills, and I took care of your ungrateful ass for seventeen years."

"Bye, Ma."

Claudia waved her off and disappeared from the doorway.

Shaking her head and displaying a similar grin, Tesla set her purse down on the dresser. Debbie sat in the swivel chair in front of Claudia's computer desk in the far left corner of the room. Lorenzo stood leaning back against the dresser, arms folded across his thickly muscled chest, eyes fixed on Tesla as she lifted five packets of bank-new hundreds out of her croc skin Birkin and stacked them neatly beside it. His gaze shifted to the fifty-thousand-dollar mound of Crips Benjamins and lingered there for several seconds.

"Remember what I told you, Zo. I don't want you spending this on another old-ass-car. Get yourself something nice, something that didn't come out before we did. You got three daughters, a niece, and two nephews. Get one of those Expeditions. If you absolutely have to get a car, get a Benz, an E-Class or an S-Class."

Debbie said, "I can help him get it. My girl's aunt works at a luxury car lot. I was just telling your mom about it."

Tesla turned her full attention to Debbie, intent on interrogating the stranger, but just then Debbie's cell phone – a cheap-looking Nokia-buzzed, and Debbie answered the call. Apparently it was Debbie's mother, fretting over last night's robbery.

Turning back to Lorenzo, Tesla instinctively shot a glance at the front of his sweatpants, seeking his signature cock-bulge. Unfortunately, the sweats were too loose-fitting. She could not discern even the slightest phallic outline.

Raising her eyes to meet his, she caught the knowing look on his disturbingly handsome face and struggled to repress an eye-roll. She wrinkled her nose at him in an idiosyncratic grimace of feigned disgust.

"I think I might know somebody who can put you on," she said. "I'm not all the way sure yet, but I might be able to hook you up with a connect. I'm working on it."

"Is that car really yours?"

"Of course it's mine. You know I only drive what I own. Mama didn't raise no fool. That Range Rover's mine too."

"You got it like that now, huh? Young millionaire."

"I ain't no millionaire. I'm doing okay for myself, but I ain't no millionaire. I will be – as soon as I get my clothing line off the ground."

"Your man got a billi and you ain't even got a milli?"

Tesla's easygoing expression became contemptuous. "Worry about your own relationship," she said tightly.

"Make that nigga run you that check. Tell him you need a couple million to get your shit together." He picked up the pile of cash and used his thumb to fan through it. "I ain't tryna get all up in your–"

"Yes, you are. Yes-the-hell you are. You're being nosy instead of being grateful for me going outta my way to help your ungrateful ass."

Lorenzo grinned. It was a real stupid fucking grin, in Tesla's opinion. Odd how she'd once loved that idiotic grin. Now, at this moment, he loathed it.

"My bad," he said.

"Damn right it's your bad."

Debbie ended her call, took off her shades, and began composing a text message. She said, "I'm texting Shanita. We should be able to go straight to the dealership. I think you should get the S550. either that or a G-Wagon like the one Claudia got out there." She looked up from her phone, and Tesla saw that she looked even more attractive without the sunglasses. Unbelievably attractive. "Oh, my God. My mama is so extra. She was about to hit the highway with the whole Hicks family."

Still grinning like a complete fool, Lorenzo stuffed the cash into his sweatpants pockets and admired the impressive bulges the stacks made. "Racks!" He said triumphantly.

"Don't spend any of it on dope," Tesla said.

"I don't need to. Prince heard about what happened last night and front me a whole chicken. I got the trap jumpin' right now. Whipped that thirty six into a hard forty-two. Got the trap on Bouldercrest and the trap in Bankhead doin' numbers. I'm good. Real niggas don't fall off. I put too many real niggas on when I had it. The streets got me like I got them."

Lo, also called Shawty Lo, was a mostly behind the scenes member of Dem Franchize Boyz, a rap group from Bowen Homes. Their 2003 hit record "White Tee" was still in heavy rotation on the radio. The group was currently busy touring the country, but Lo rarely made appearances with them. He was a ghetto millionaire on the low, by far the most successful paths with him at a huge Independence Day party he'd thrown in the hood, and they'd had a threesome with him in a suite at the Four Seasons later that night. He'd paid them fifteen hundred dollars apiece for the good time. Afterward, Tesla had lain next to him, ogling the sparkling white diamond baguettes in his bracelet, wristwatch, and necklaces while he answered phone calls from hood bitches and street niggas all across the South. She'd made him promise no to tell anyone about their sexual encounter, mainly because she didn't want word getting back to Lorenzo, but also because at the time she'd been two weeks into what ended up being a nine-week relationship with Isaac Bolton, rookie wide receiver for the Tennessee Titans.

"Lo's a good dude," Tesla said neutrally. "I'm just glad Rari wasn't with you when y'all got robbed. I would've lost it."

"What's up with that plug you just mentioned?" Lorenz asked, lighting a Newport.

"I'm not even sure he is a plug yet. He might be, he might not be. I'll find out soon enough, and when I do I'll let you know. Can you stay out of all the street shit until then? Please?"

"That's like asking a fat nigga to stay out the kitchen."

"Do you see a smile on my face? I'm trying to make things better for all of us. I don't want my daughter growing up without a father."

Debbie stood up. "I'll keep him in check. If he don't listen to me we can jump his ass. Or I'll beat his ass by myself?"

Beaming, Tesla walked around to the other side of the bed and gave Debbie a high-five. She said, "That's what it is. Fuck him up. And if he hits you back, call me asap. I'll drive right the fuck over there."

The two girls smiled, nodding their heads slowly and menacingly. Lorenzo chuckled and puffed on his cigarettes.

"Debbie, don't let Tesla get you beat up," he said.

"Don't fuck around and get beat up," Debbie countered.

Lorenzo's eighteen-year-old cousin Derek, better known as Bo Jangles or just plain Bo, stepped into the doorway with one hand buried in a big bag of Flamin' Hot Cheetos. Even with the huge t-shirt he had on, his fat ball of a belly protruded. He wasn't morbidly obese just yet, but he was well on his way. His skin was dark like Lorenzo's, and he was six foot four. He'd been the star linebacker of his high school football team, with scholarships from a dozen colleges. Then he'd taken two gunshots to the leg and one to the stomach when his girlfriend's side nigga caught him slipping one night last October, and his dreams of becoming a professional athlete went out the window. No, he was just another street nigga from Bankhead, doing whatever he needed to do to keep food on his table and a roof over his head. A couple of weeks ago, he'd been detained and questioned about the side nigga's recent murder. Five days before that, he'd been caught with three pounds of weed and four and a half ounces of cocaine in the trunk of his Pontiac Bonneville. Tesla had put $5,000 toward his bail; he was her daughter's godfather.

Zo stepped out to the living room with Bo. Tesla rushed to the door, threw it shut, and engaged the lock. "Fuck him. Let's girl-talk. Tell me about last night. Who do you think was behind the robbery?" Debbie swore that she had no idea who might have been responsible for the armed robbery and carjacking. While she filled Tesla in on what had gone down at around two o'clock this morning, Tesla studied the girl's sexy features: the smoldering brown eyes, rendered bloodshot from marijuana consumption; the immaculately groomed eyebrows; the thick-lipped, sugary smile that had yet to leave her perfect reddish brown face; the globular gold tongue ring that twinkled in the shafts of sunlight splitting in through the venetian blinds. Tesla wondered if Debbie's pussy was just as pretty as the rest of her body. During her two and a half years as a stripper, Tesla had enjoyed numerous lesbian encounters, and although she considered herself heterosexual, she didn't mind dabbling on the other side every now and then. Especially when the girl on the other side looked like Debbie.

" … and then they pushed me to the ground and took all my jewelry," Debbie was saying. She had sat down again, and she was speaking in earnest. "Got me using this cheap ass phone. I wish I did know who was behind that shit. I'd pull upon them myself."

"I'll ask around and see if I can find out something."

"Please do. I need my stuff back. Your girl Juicy said she would ask around too, but I think she might've told me that just to get in good with me. She was giving me the look, if you know what I mean, and she gave me her number when we stopped to get these new phones. Don't get me wrong, I like girls and all, but she picked the wrong time to be trying to flirt."

"You like girls?" Tesla asked, struggling to suppress her excitement.

Debbie nodded. "More than I like men, actually. I've been in relationships with girls. To be honest, a man has never even given me an orgasm. It might be because I've only dated younger men. They way the older men, men in their thirties and forties, know how to get the job done."

"Not just the older men," Tesla said, thinking of Diego. "You might need to look outside your race. My man is Colombian and Brazilian. He eats me for hours. Mmm. I tremble just thinking about it."

"Does he stay on the clit, though? Because a lot of men … you know … they like to lick all in the hole. Which does nothing for me."

"Oh, no. My boo knows where to put that tongue to work. He does lick inside every now and then, but mostly he focuses on the clitoris." Tesla walked around the large bed and sat down on the soft Versace comforter. Debbie was just across from her. "Okay, Debbie, we need to quit talking about getting head. I popped an ecstasy pill early this morning and I think it's still in my system."

"Your man got a brother?" Debbie asked in a conspiratorial tone.

"He does, but he wouldn't be interested in you. Jorge is gay. Dresses like a girl and everything. He lives somewhere in Bogota, Colombia. His daddy cut him off when he came out the closet."

"Is your guy really a billionaire?"

Tesla hesitated. She didn't like revealing too much about Diego's wealth. Bitches were far too treacherous. Nobody respects relationships these days. As long as a man had money, most of the girls Tesla knew would sleep with him no matter who he was dating. "He's well off," she said finally. "I don't believe he's a billionaire. Who told you that?"

"Juicy told Zo and Kilo all about him." "Oh, really?"

"Yeah. She told them about the Las Vegas suite and the private jet. Not to be all up in your relationship, but I agree with Juicy. You shouldn't be giving up the goodies to somebody that rich without at least getting a ring put on your finger. I mean, imagine how dumb you'd look if he broke it off today, only to see him at the altar three or four months later with a new chick.

"I doubt that," Tesla said noncommittally.

"Girl, you better put some safeguards in place. Like my granny always say, 'Ain't no sense in buying the cow when you can get the milk for free,' and I feel her on that one. If I was in your shoes, I would rush him into a marriage. Quick. You know why?" She paused briefly as someone on the opposite side of the bedroom door attempted to turn the doorknob, then sailed on, her tongue ring twinkling in the light as she spoke. "I would be sicker than a stage-four cancer patient with the flu if some random bitch married him after me and got what was rightfully mine. What if the next bitch marries him, divorces him nine or ten years later, and leaves the marriage with five hundred million dollars? How would you feel about that?"

Tesla had no words. The insecurities she'd buried way down in the depths of her mind long ago began digging themselves out like the skeletal fingers of the undead in an old horror movie. She was already suspicious of Diego's involvement with his ex-girlfriend. And why hadn't he returned her calls? She'd phoned him twice, back to back. He usually returned her calls within minutes.

Just then, almost as if he had implanted some sort of spyware in her head that alerted him to her very thoughts, her Nextel rang with a call from Diego. She got up and sauntered to the door, flipping open the phone and snatching up her purse as she went. She told Debbie it was an important call as she unlocked the door, pulled it open, and stalked past the sofa where Lorenzo and his cousin Bo were seated with beers in hand. "One second," she said into the phone. She went out to the sunporch and stood amongst a bevy of haphazardly stacked cardboard boxes, gazing out the tinted windows at her sleek black Ferrari.

"Are you in California?" She said, holding the cell phone to her ear.

"No. I'm home ... waiting for you."

"And it took you this long to return my calls?"

"I apologize for that. Had an important meeting. Where'd you go?"

Tesla clucked her tongue. "I'm a good woman, you know that. A damned good one. I'm not about to keep waiting for you to make it official. If you don't see us being together for the long run, tell me now."

"What do you mean? You're my girlfriend."

"Yeah, but you should want me to be more than a girlfriend. You should want me to be your wife." Tears welled up in her eyes. She realized she was shouting into the phone and instantly regretted it.

Diego paused for a long moment. "Who have you been listening to?" He asked, after a time. "Your mother? One of your friends?"

"Nobody," she lied, sniffling.

"You talked to somebody. Who was it?"

"Just forget it, Diego." "A few weeks ago you told me you wanted to wait until you were twenty-five to get married.

Now all of a sudden you want to get married. You talked to somebody, and I'm willing to bet they put some foolish idea in your head. Probably told you to force an engagement before another woman comes along and takes your place. Am I right or am I right?"

Tesla snickered softly, thumbing away the tears. "Shut up talking to me, Diego."

He laughed. "I knew it."

"You didn't know jack shit."

"Listen, if you want to be my fiancé, if you want me to go out and get you the most magnificent engagement ring I can find and propose to you in the most amazing way imaginable, I'll do that."

"Good. Then do it."

Chapter 9

Diego was in his home office on a conference call with Craig Ross and Andrew Lipsay, operations heads of Santos Prime Properties' New York City and London offices, when one of the high-tech flex screen camera monitors forming a semicircular shield around the font of his large mahogany desk started flashing red. One of the motion sensing exterior cameras outside the Casa Grande's towering black wrought iron front gates had picked up movement. He looked up at the screen and saw that Tesla's shiny black Ferrari and her Range Rover were idling in tandem outside the gates, waiting to be let in.

The distance from the front gates (which were monogrammed with Diego's initials) to the main house was approximately ninety-five yards. The rolling lawns that flanked the long driveway were rich with expensive Bermuda grass. Diego watched the two luxury vehicles as they entered the slowly opening gates, proceeded up the driveway, and parked on the side of the vast parking area where his own two luxury vehicles – identical blacked-out Rolls Royce Phantoms – sat. The vehicles parked at the opposite end of the lot, near the guard shack, were all SUVs: four black Cadillac Escalades, four black Chevy Suburban's, and the blacked-out Hummer limo. All but the limo was mostly used by the help and the bodyguards.

Diego ended the conference call seconds before Tesla walked into his office. She had a guilty smirk on her face, an expectant sparkle in her eyes.

"Go ahead," she said. "Cuss me out. I deserve it." She had a twenty-ounce bottle of Mountain Dew in one hand, the arches of her purse straps in the other. She elbowed the heavy door shut and sauntered across the room to him.

"Where's your daughter?" Diego asked, turning in his plushy upholstered white leather swivel chair as Tesla joined him behind his desk. He'd changed into a fresh navy Armani suit, and tie, because the suit he'd worn earlier was splattered with blood. Under his desk, Diamante was curled into a heap, taking a doggie nap.

"I left her with my mama. She wanted to stay and play with Marlana, and I don't really want her here with me anyway. Not when you got people trying to kill your ex." She set her purse down next to his glass of water and took a drink from her own beverage. "You need to tell me what's going on. I mean what's *really* going on. And before you get to grazing over the facts, please know that I've already done my own little investigation. I know all about your father's connections to the Colombian cartel."

Diego sat back and studied Tesla for a moment, resting his elbows on the armrests, steepling his fingers in front of him. Tesla was a paragon of female beauty, indisputably the most beautiful woman Diego had ever been involved with sexually. She put down her Mountain Dew and placed her hands on her waist, leaning her hip against the desk, eyeing him through squinted lids.

He had greatly underestimated her intelligence, he realized. Somehow, some way, she had discovered a facade-shattering truth about his father without ever having met the man. It was an eye opening realization. If Tesla had figured it out already, how many others knew?

"Listen, Diego," she said gravely, "because I'm only gonna say this once. Either you tell me the truth or I'm going back to doing me. Yoshi already has me booked for an event at Strokers tonight that's paying thirty grand. I'm not about to keep staying in this stagnant situation, hardly making any money at all while you lie to my face about what's really goin' on. Tell me the truth."

"You want the truth?"

"Yes, I want the truth, the whole truth, and nothing but the truth." Diego stood up and turned to the large, 24-karat-gold framed painting that hung on the wall behind his desk. It was a portrait of his parents at the altar, drawn from an actual wedding photo by a prominent Colombian painter whose life had long since expired from a heroin overdose. Diego grabbed the painting at the bottom corners of the frame and hoisted it upward. It slid up the wall on a pair of widely spaced parallel tracks, revealing the big square door of a stainless steel wall safe with a numbered keypad at its center. He punched in the six-digit code, 091204, the date of his and Tesla's first encounter six months ago. The door opened automatically, with a pneumatic hiss and a single beep. Tesla peered into the safe, and her brow shot to the top of her forehead as she peered in. There was exactly $4.7 million in there, four neat rows across and three rows back, bank-new hundred-dollar bills piled almost to the steel ceiling.

"The truth is," Diego said, looking at Tesla, "you're not going to be at Strokers tonight. No tonight, not tomorrow night – not ever again. No more taking off your clothes and dancing to make ends meet. I told you this months ago."

She peeled her captivating green eyes off the cash and settled them on Diego's intense gray ones. He tried to imagine what it must be like inside that head of hers. What thoughts consumed her waking hours? What dreams came to her at night? She told him some things, but he wanted to know more.

"I saw your password," she said.

"Wasn't trying to hide it. It's the date we met, September twelfth of last year. Best day of my life." He sat down and drank some water. "There's close to five million in there. Take whatever you need, whenever you need it. Just … no more stripping."

"Who said anything about stripping? It's a hosting—"

"Whatever it is, don't do it. From here on out, at least for the next year or so, I need you by my side every waking hour of the day. We go out together. We eat together. We exercise together. I need someone who genuinely loves me in my corner. I've just entered a rather precarious stage in my life, and I need you to be my extra set of eyes and ears."Tesla folded her arms under her breasts, stuck out her lower lip, and sighed through her nose. "Tell me what's going on. And please remember that most of my exes are gangstas and drug-dealers. I know how to keep my mouth shut."

This time it was Diego who sighed. He took a sip of water and drew his lips thin. Could he really come clean to Tesla about his role in the Barranquilla cartel? He considered himself a fairly good judge of character. Tesla, in his opinion, was loyal and trustworthy. He didn't want to embroil her in the perils of cartel life, but he couldn't very well leave her in the dark. She needed to understand the risks of being the spouse of a future cartel boss and what to do if she was ever taken in by state or federal authorities for questioning.

Picking up on his hesitation, Tesla shifted her weight to the other leg and lifted her brow, a telltale sign of impatience.

"Okay," Diego said resignedly. "Okay. I'll tell you. But first you have to promise to keep your lips absolutely sealed. Nothing I say leaves this room. We clear on that? Nothing."

"I'm listening."

Reluctantly, he began laying out the truth. Most of it, at least. He told her about the significance of his new pinkie ring, revealed to her that he was an upper echelon Colombian drug cartel member, essentially the underboss, and that soon he would be the boss. He explained to her that the assassination of Camila's finance had been carried out by the Mara Salvatrucha Trese, or MS-13, but that they were merely pawns in the grand scheme of it all. The order had come from the very top of the food chain, if not from his cantankerous supermodel sister then probably from the boss of some other drug cartel.

"Wait a minute," Tesla said. "So you mean to tell me that your sister, the same girl I see in all the magazines and TV commercials, is actually a drug cartel member?"

Diego nodded. "And I may be wrong, but I'm pretty sure she's the one who had Camila's boyfriend killed. We're checking into it now. I believe she ordered the hit because she said bad things about you and I gave her an ultimatum. Either she apologizes to you or I send some guys to mam her boyfriend. I think that pissed her off." he saw the confused look on Tesla's face and added, "she and I aren't exactly the best of friends. She feels like control of the cartel should go to her, not me. Her way of expressing her dissent is violence. No thanks to Popeye."

"Popeye?"

"John 'Popeye' Velasquez. He was Pablo Escobar's hitman, a close friend of my father's, too. Taught me and Sofia everything he knew during our summer breaks from school in West Palm Beach. We'd fly down to Medellin and spend three or four weeks with him, perfecting our aim at the gun range, learning hand-to-hand combat techniques. Grueling work, but I appreciated the training. Sofia took to it better and faster than I did. Our father cancelled the training sessions after one of Sofia's high school rivals was found dead in the girls' restroom. The girl had been killed with a hunting knife in the exact way Popeye had just taught us. It's called a Colombian necktie. You slit the person's throat and pull their tongue out through the slit."

"Wow." Tesla sounded stunned. "She actually got away with that?"

"Was never even a suspect." Tesla became thoughtful. Arms crossed, she turned her back to the desk and let it all sink in, regarding the cash in the wall safe with a thousand-yard stare.

Meantime, Diego was unable to keep his gaze from momentarily shifting to her fat round posterior. He was, unapologetically, an ass-man, had been ever since he was a mild-mannered Floridian teen gallivanting with his Black friends in South Florida. It had begun in the summer of 1999, when Miami rapper Trina first burst onto the scene with her sexually charged lyrics and bootylicious choreography. Then Diego had fallen for Free, the co-host of BET's 106th and Park, and that was all she wrote. From then on he'd been attracted to nothing but pretty girls with big butts. Camila, the porn star Heather Medine, and Tesla were all gorgeous women with beautiful meaty butts, though Tesla's was much thicker than the former two. She was also much more attractive than any girl he'd ever slept with.

"A'ight," Tesla said finally. The perturbed look was gone. In its place was a dim smirk. She nodded her head in agreement with whatever she was thinking. "I want in. Not for me – for my brother Marlan when he comes home, and for Rari's daddy. They're both used to moving bricks."

"I'm not letting you get involved with any sort of drug-trafficking."

"I don't want to get involved. I just want them to have a real plug, so they can take care of their kids. Just in case anything ever happens to me."

Shaking his head no, Diego stood up and pushed the door of the safe shut. The painting came down automatically. "We'll discuss this later," he said. "Let's go. I have something to show you."

The two of them sat abreast in the back of Diego's Phantom, Tesla with Diamante nestled in her lap, Diego with his Nextel to his ear. He must have received some kind of good news. He seemed excited. Just as the spacious sedan exited the front gates with two SUVs trailing in tandem behind it, Tesla began to wonder what her older sister Nikola was up to in Chicago. Nikola was a year older than Tesla. She lived with her husband, Anthony Baldwin, and their two small children. Anthony was a club promoter, Nikola a college student and part-time school teacher. Both Atlanta natives, the couple had packed up and moved to the Windy City four years ago to live in an apartment building Anthony's maternal grandmother had left him in her will.

Nikola and Tesla had a notoriously volatile relationship, which is why Tesla sort of understood Diego and his sister's bitter rivalry. The Harrison sisters had spent half their childhood at odds with each other over the stupidest things. Clothes, boys, personal space, hair care products, best friends. Practically everything was cause for war, and when they weren't fighting each other it was usually because they were teaming up to fight other girls.

The final straw had come shortly before Nikola and Anthony's sudden departure from Atlanta, when Anthony took Tesla, Rhonda, and Stacy to see Aaliyah live in concert, leaving his then nine-month pregnant girlfriend Nikola at home. Shortly after leaving the show, they stopped at a White Castle, and while Stacy and Rhonda went inside the restaurant to use the restroom and to order their meals Anthony and Tesla sat smoking a blunt and talking in the car. The conversation had gone from Anthony's admiration for Sean "Puffy" Combs, a club promoter turned music mogul, to his unwavering lust for Puffy's ex Jennifer Lopez. Which somehow led to him confessing that he'd also had a crush on Tesla.

Tesla deeply regretted what happened next. Anthony had coaxed her into joining him in the backseat of his 1993 Chevy Caprice, where the two of them committed the ultimate betrayal. The guilt of what she'd done had weighed heavily on Tesla's conscience for days afterward until finally she came clean to her mother, who then broke the news to Nikola.

Since then the two sisters had not spoken to each other. Not even once. Not during the moving process when Tesla helped load the moving truck, not last year when Nikola received an associates degree from Loyola, not even this past November when Nikola and Anthony flew in for Thanksgiving. It was an unfortunate situation that Tesla often found herself crying over.

Diego flipped his phone shut, ending his call. He took one look at Tesla and immediately sensed her dejection. "What's wrong?" He asked, expression shifting from one of elation to one of empathy.

Tesla shook her head. "Nothing." She went on scratching and rubbing Diamante's back as he lay on his side with his tongue out.

"Well, I've got great news— on two fronts, actually. SPP now has all the permits required to build a new tower of condominiums in Rochester, New York. Our team of lawyers have been fighting for years to get that approval. Years. We were battling with Donald Trump's attorneys over that particular lot of land." Diego's elated expression returned. He reached over and gave Tesla's knee a gentle squeeze. "Speaking of attorneys, if you're ever arrested or interrogated by any police or federal agents, ask for your lawyer and don't say anything else. The only info you give them is what's on your ID, your name and date of birth. All other questions are to be directed to your lawyer, Dulce Gordoa. If I'm ever arrested, do the same thing. Call Gordoa. Hand me your phone, I'll lock in her number."

"What's the second front?" Tesla asked, handing over her phone. "You said you had great news on two fronts."

"Oh." Diego pressed a button on the console between their seats, and a black glass partition rose behind the driver's seat, efficiently blocking them off from the driver's view and earshot. "I love the partition feature. It's only available in the extended-wheelbase models."

Tesla turned to look at him. Her eyes were narrow slits.

"Right," he said. The second front."

"Don't play with me, Diego. Please don't."

"Okay, okay," he said, chuckling good-naturedly. "We, uh … we have a fleet of multimillion-dollar subma – whoa, wait a second. Another thing. Never discuss anything illegal over the phone or through text messages. Never discuss any drug deals or incoming drug shipments with anyone. Never even mention the Barranquilla cartel or what goes on within the Barranquilla cartel to anyone but me and Lazaro."

"Rhonda already knows. She's the one who found it online and told me about it."

"Oh, that's nothing. That means she only knows what the Feds *think* they know. I could care less about that dead journalist, and those investigators in Mexico. They got what they deserved, you ask me," Diego said, twisting and turning the ring on his pinkie finger. "Anyway, we have a fleet of submarines that, uhh …" He hesitated, still twisting the ring. Thinking tentatively, he continued, "We usually ship everything to Mexico, in airplanes or eighteen-wheelers, but for the larger shipments we use submarines. Usually the submarines surface off the coast of Mexico, in La Paz or Mazatlan or Acapulco, but every once in a while we managed to get one to the California coastline, or up through the Gulf of Mexico to Corpus Christi or Galveston, Texas."

"Can't those be tracked by radar?"

"No. they're stealth subs, specifically designed to avoid radar detection. The U.S. is working on developing technology to combat that sort of trafficking, but for now they depend mostly on aerial surveillance and confidential informants to crack down on what goes on underwater. Laz must have called my pops and done some serious ass-kissing, because we have one on the way. Seventy-five hundred kilos of uncut perico. The purest cocaine on the market."

Tesla gaped at Diego, momentarily at a loss for words. She made a mental attempt to calculate the astronomical sum of cash that seventy-five hundred kilos of coke could bring in, but she was too stunned to do the math.

"Jesus Christ," she muttered. It took her a moment to get her mind back into gear. Her first priority was securing her daughter's future, which meant that both of Ferrari's parents needed to become financially stable and stay that way. "Enzo can move bricks, and so can my brother. I say you get somebody to front them ten or fifteen bricks a piece."

Diego was already shaking his head. "No, no, no," he said. "I'll get your brother into something legitimate. Or at least something that won't get him a lifetime in some fed joint if he's ever busted. I have a job for him when he comes home."

For a moment, Tesla sat staring at the lawyer's mobile number in her phone's contacts list, thinking of all the hardships she'd endure over the years, all the laps she'd danced on and shiny chromium poles she'd swung around to finally get to this point. And what exactly was this point? She had a rich boyfriend – not a rich fiancé, not a rich husband, a rich boyfriend. What if Debbie was right? What if Diego got tired of her in the near future? What if he humped her and moved on to the next bitch? She truly did love him, but was she letting love blind her to the common sense approach she needed to be taking to secure her daughter's future? She wasn't sure.

"What's wrong?" Diego asked for the second time. "Don't lie and tell me it's nothing. I have a pretty good intuition."

She looked up from her cell phone, folding it shut and dropping it in her purse and gazing into Diego's inquisitive eyes. "What happened between you and Camila? Why didn't it work out?" She asked.

"It didn't work out because I prefer the strength and beauty of a girl from the slums. Camila was my type physically, but she's too innocent. I like hood girls. Tough girls. All my closest friends from Florida are Black guys, and not the preppy kind. My guy Mark's cousin was Chubb, founder of Miami's Zoe Pound. Pops bought me a G-Wagon for my sixteenth birthday. A lot of Fridays me, Mark, and the boys would hop in the G-Wagon and drive down to Miami. We'd hang out in Little Haiti with Chubb, Macka Zoe, Ali Adam. the whole Zoe Pound. Those guys had guns lying around everywhere, kilos of coke and pounds of weed, nineteen seventy-three Chevy Caprices on dubs. We'd have parties with celebrities. DJ Khaled, The Refugees, Trick Daddy. All the hood girls would come out to party with us. I knew right away that Camila wasn't for me, and she knew it too. So we broke up, went our separate ways, but we've always remained friends."

Tesla narrowed her eyes at him. "A'ight, now. Don't get too friendly with that bitch."

"I should be telling you not to get too friendly with Lorenzo. You were alone with him and his girlfriend, in your mom's bedroom. Gave him fifty grand."

Tesla gasped and froze in her seat, eyes wide, mouth open. How had he found out so quickly? Were there hidden cameras in her mother's bedroom.?

"Yeah," Diego said, smiling, clearly enjoying the moment. "Didn't think I'd find out, did you? I talked to your mom a few minutes after you left her house. She told me everything. The ten grand you gave her when she returned from the liquor store, the fifty you gave Lorenzo."

The corners of Tesla's mouth rose slowly to form a guilty, open-mouthed smile. "I hate snitches," she said. "But for the record, nothing happened. I wouldn't touch him with a ten foot pole. He got robbed for basically everything he had last night, including his car. He's done a lot for me financially. I'm just returning the favor."

"As long as you keep things platonic, I really don't mind you helping him get his life together. I'd do the same for Camila in a heartbeat."

A flood of relief washed through Tesla. Diego knew about the money she'd given Lorenzo and he wasn't upset about it. Her tentative smile became a genuinely happy one. She leaned in to him, kissed him on the lips, twice.

"I love you so much," she murmured sweetly.

"You'll love me even more in a minute," he replied.

It was actually seven minutes later when the Rolls-Royce came to a halt. Tesla had no idea where they were. Curtains were drawn shut over her and Diego's windows, and the partition ahead of them was pitch black. She started to turn and look out the darkly tinted rear window, but then her door was pulled open. It was a rear-hinged door, opening from the front. Diego's door swung out at the same instant.

Tesla stepped out and looked around. She recognized the location. They were in front of what used to be Club Gold. only now it was no longer the single-story building it once was. Sometime last year, Club Gold had been demolished. What now stood in its place was a beautiful two-story building made of Graystone and glass. A red-on-black sign high up on the left side of the building displayed the name of the newborn establishment. Tesla had seen the building twice in recent weeks, but the sign was new. Her eyes got big as she read the name aloud.

"Tesla's," she murmured in disbelief.

Also on the sign were the silhouettes of two women, one midway up a pole, the other squatting below. To the right of that was a list of what the building offered to the community: FOOD, DRINKS, EXOTIC DANCERS, 1-ON-1 SHOWS.

Off to the right of the building was a large parking lot, in the near right corner of which was an almost identical sign at the top of a tall black pole, only this sign was at least twice as large and included a phone number. The parking lot extended around the rear of the building, where there was a second vehicular entrance/exit.

There were three vehicles sitting in the parking lot, a black Cadillac limousine and two of the blacked-out Escalades the maids and bodyguards were known to drive.

Tesla stuck out her tongue, yelled, and laughed all at the same time. She put the dog down and leapt into Diego's arms as he joined her on the sidewalk. Jumped right up and wrapped her legs around his waist, her arms around his neck. She kissed him eight or nine times in a row, shrieking an elated "Thank you!" between each kiss.

"Now you'll have your own strip club to own and operate. One here, one in Miami, and another one in Philadelphia. This one has over ten thousand square feet of floor space," Diego said as Tesla lowered her feet to the ground. "The other two are still under construction, but this one's ready for business."

"And they're all mine?"

"Technically, we're co-owners, but in reality they're all yours. The liquor license is in my name. There's a lot of paperwork you need to look over and sign, to make it all official. You'll need to hire bouncers and bartenders and hold auditions for dancers. I'll help you with all that."

Sensing the excitement above, Diamante stood barking with his hind legs slightly bent, ready to pounce. We fell in step beside Tesla as Diego took her hand in his and led her towards the pair of opaque glass doors that Diego's two main bodyguards, Lee and Max, were holding open. Tesla looked up at the red-on-black awning that hung over the open doorways and saw the possessive form of her name yet again. Tesla's written in lustrous cursive lettering, just like on the signs.

Entering the strip club, Tesla gave the lobby a cursory glance. There was a high wooden desk off to the left that reminded her of the kind of hotel receptionists sat behind. A pair of walk-through metal detectors stood side by side in the middle of the smooth black marble floor. The bottom halves of the walls were made of the same gold-veined black marble, the top halves of red oak paneling. There were two open doors behind the desk, one revealing a restroom, the other a long wooden table lined with camera monitors. To her right were two more doors, closed, and a roped-off hallway that led to a staircase. The placard hanging from the wrinkled red velvet rope read VIP ONLY. beyond the metal detectors were two large red doors, also closed. Tesla discerned movement in the narrow windows of the big red doors.

They continued onward, Diego beaming coolly in his conservative business suit, Tesla trembling with excitement in her Gucci ensemble. Max pulled open one of the big red doors, and all of a sudden Tesla screamed a very happy scream, sending Diamantic into yet another barking fit as she took off running through the doorway.

It was the sight of her family that cranked up Tesla's level of excitement, the sight of her friends that sent her running. Claudia, Rari, and Marlana; Aunt Thelma Harrison, her four adult children, and their eight teenage children; Rhonda and her on-again boyfriend Darius Carter, a New York Times best-selling novelist she'd met at last year's Essence Festival' Juicy and her twins. They were all standing around a table with toothy smiles on their faces. There was a three-tiered cake with brightly burning sparklers on the table.

"Congratulations!" Everyone yelled in complete unison, as if they had rehearsed the congratulatory shout beforehand.

Then came the most shocking surprise of all.

Tesla felt a tug on the back of her shirt. She turned around to find her boyfriend down on one knee. The open black box resting in the palm of his hand held the most gorgeous – and undoubtedly the most expensive – diamond ring Tesla had ever seen. The stone was gigantic and set in platinum.

Rhonda's camera was flashing away as Tesla, nodding her head rapidly and fighting back tears of joy, gave Diego the big "Yes!"

Chapter 10

Snowfall was much more than the sum of its parts. Alvaro had commissioned world-renowned luxury yacht-maker Benetti to build the superyacht four days after the horrific 9/11 terrorist attacks, often phoning Benetti CEO Vincenzo Poerio several times a week during the three-year construction phase to keep track of its progress. Benetti had done a sublime job, creating a clean profile by layering the five decks plus subdeck of the 238-foot exterior while also using smart contemporary design for external social areas. The foredeck doubled as a private gathering area, with an alfresco dining room under a specially designed tent. The beach club had an espresso bar where guests could enjoy water views. A gym was located on the upper deck, and the main deck housed a hair salon, massage tables, and a fold-down balcony. Snowfall also had a 26,000-gallon glass-bottomed pool on the main deck, plus a Jacuzzi on the sundeck and an outdoor cinema on the owner's deck. Toys included a sailing catamaran, a ski boat, and five Jet Skies, and there was a helipad on the top deck.

The superyacht's interior was elegant and informal: Douglas fir and lime oak were the primary woods, while forty other materials helped customize the saloons and eight staterooms.

Diego was lying poolside in a red-cushioned lounge chair, cooling in the shade of an oversized umbrella of the same color. The sixteen lounge chairs flanking the swimming pool were paired up in twos, paired so closely that the two essentially became one. Tesla occupied the one next to Diego. She was admiring the 35-carat D flawless white diamond on her sixteen-million-dollar Harry Winston engagement ring, a big smile fixed on her stunning pie-shaped visage. She had on a red D&G bikini. Her hair was done up in a messy topknot.

Five weeks had passed since Diego's surprising strip club proposal. In the weeks since, he'd managed to successfully smuggled 7,550 kilograms of cocaine into the United States via fully submersible submarine; he and Tesla had begun the daunting process of furnishing their new home, a 15,000-square-foot mansion on a four-acre promontory in Malibu, California; he'd tracked down the MS-13 leader in Los Angeles and confirmed what he'd known all along, that Sofia had hired the MS-13 gang to murder Camila's fiancé; and, just last night, he'd had eight hundred pounds of hydroponic marijuana and fifty kilograms of Mexican heroin sent through a subterranean drug tunnel that ran from a horse farm in Tijuana to the laundry room in a ranch-style estate in San Diego.

The coke was moving fast. A thousand kilos had gone to the Ruiz brothers in Chicago. They were identical twins with ties to the Latin Kings and several other Hispanic street gangs. Twelve hundred kilos had gone to Miami – half to Zoe Pound, the other half to the Carol City Cartel. Diego had befriended the top dogs in both crews years ago, and they'd been reliable ever since he got his first major load of blow into the country. Eight hundred kilos had gone to Bundy, the flamboyant kid out of D.C. half paid for, half on consignment, had paid $3.6 million cash for three hundred kilos. (Diego had lowered the wholesale price of his kilos to $12,000 a piece to undercut the competition). He'd sent thirty kilos to a crew of Bloods in Cincinnati, a hundred to a Dominican drug boss in Philly, forty to a reliable Harlem kingpin.

Against his better judgement, Diego had gotten fifty kilos into Lorenzo's hands. He'd had Lazaro send the bricks to Lorenzo' Zone 1 trap house. Lorenzo would pay just $10,000 per kilo, none of it up front. Diego had done it for Rari, really; God knew how much he loved that little girl. Plus he knew it would keep Lorenzo busy and away from Tesla.

Alejandro Romero and his MS-13 crew had their own clientele. They'd moved a hundred and twenty bricks the first week, two hundred the second week, and they were currently working through two hundred more. Four hundred pounds of the hydroponic marijuana that had come through the drug tunnel was going to them, the other four hundred to the Ruiz brothers.

Yes. things were going great. Diego had given Camila $50,000 to finance her fiancé's funeral, and now she was back in South Florida, living with her two older sisters in one of Diego's Miami mansions. Tesla was in a good space. She hadn't stopped smiling ever since the proposal. She'd hired a full staff of waitresses and bartenders to run her strip club, a security team to keep out uncouth troublemakers and protect the dancers, and a kitchen crew to keep staff and patrons fed and hydrated. She'd put together an all-star lineup of thickly-proportioned exotic dancers, a third of whom were New York City transplants who'd responded to an ad she had placed on a West Brooklyn billboard. She and her brother Marlan, who'd been released from Fulton County jail just last week and would manage the club when it opened tomorrow night, had sat through three days of exciting auditions this week, and now Marlan was out in the water on a Jet Ski with Sparkle, one of the girls he'd met at the second audition.

Tesla went from ogling the ring to staring at Diego. "Can life get any better than this?" She asked.

"I don't think so," he said. He looked in her eyes and saw his own joy reflected there. Their hands found each other, holding fast to a moment the two of them were likely never to forget.

Snowfall was anchored in the Straits of Florida's glorious blue waters, about twenty miles southeast of Miami. The superyacht had a crew of twenty-two including the captain, Sean Gilmore, who was also Diego's pilot. Diego and Tesla had brought eight others aboard Snowfall with them. Marlan and Sparkle and Juicy. Lazaro and Adela. Anthony and Nikola. The eight of them were out leaping waves and racing around in the cool ocean water on Jet Skis, shouting and laughing, having the time of their lives.

"It's kind of a shame," Tesla said with a plaintive sigh. "My sister hadn't talked to me in years. Not even a text message. Then my mama went blabbing to her about my engagement ring and the club and all of a sudden I got a phone call. 'Congrats, lil sis! I see you!' like, what kinda bull is that? Why couldn't she reach out to me last year when I was busting my ass to take care of our whole family?"

"You're lucky she forgave you at all. Just be happy you got her back in your life. You should be glad."

"Oh, I'm glad. Don't get me wrong, I love my big sister. It's just … I hate that it took her hearing about m y blessing to finally reach out. That seems shady to me." Tesla paused, then sighed and shook her head. "You're right. Maybe I'm overanalyzing. I should just be glad to have my sister back. My baby has her auntie and two more cousins to play with. Mama said they're all holding hands and looking after each other at the amusement park."

"Sounds like fun. Now if you can keep from fucking your sister's husband – who looks like the love child of Shrek and some other hideous creature – Rari just might have a lifelong relationship with those cousins."

Diego grinned at the acerbic scowl Tesla gave him as she flipped him a middle finger. "First of all," she said, with a cobra-like sway of the head, "I didn't fuck him. I let him eat me out. There's a difference."

"I'm surprised you didn't throw up."

"I don't throw up when I'm looking down at your ugly-ass face," she countered, throwing her luscious brown legs over the side of her chair and sitting up with her back to Diego. She picked up her crystal tumbler of Louis XIII Remy Martin from the table next to her chair and drank from the straw. "I wonder what made Juicy break up with Keyvon. They were so cute together."

"Wondering about other people's problems is a complete waste of wonder," Diego said. He sat up and pressed his lips to the nape of her neck. His right hand moved almost automatically, arcing across her lounge chair, meandering up and over her right thigh, slipping down between her thighs until his fingers were so close to her pussy that the inner heat permeated her bikini bottom and warmed his knuckles. He added, "Best advice I've ever gotten was something my uncle Mateo told me on my seventeenth birthday. It's a Socrates quote: 'Strong minds discuss ideas, average minds discuss events, weak minds discuss people.' So let's discuss ideas."

"That's some real-ass shit," She said, nodding her head.

"Realest shit he ever wrote."

"That's why you're always cutting people off and asking for ideas. It's that damn Socrates quote." She stood and turned to face him in one swift motion, holding her crystal drinking glass just below her chin and sucking more champagne-cognac through the straw. She wrinkled her nose at him, her trademark expression, and said, "You ain't all that cute, you know. I think you let the whole Calvin Klein thing go to your head."

"Sounds like something a weak mind would discuss."

"Your dick game weak," She retorted wittily.

"Biggest lie you ever told." Diego grinned. He had on a pair of floral-print D&G swimming trunks and Gucci loafers. His six-pack was sharply defined, his arms and legs lean but well muscled, his skin tanned to a rich golden hue.

Snapping his fingers repeatedly, he said, "Come on. Ideas. Your strip club opens tomorrow night. What can you do to make that grand opening even grander?"

Tesla's eyes lit up. "I was just thinking about that. I mean, we already have a bunch of local celebrities and pro athletes coming through. Juicy got Lil John to DJ for opening night. Da Brat and Jermaine Dupri are coming. T.I. and Lil Wayne are performing, and they're the hottest things in the streets right now. Crime Mob and the whole Dipset are performing. Lorenzo's girlfriend is one of the baddest strippers in Atlanta, and she'll be headlining the event. It's going down. Can't even think of a way to make it any better. Not unless I get out there and dance myself."

"No," Diego said quickly. "You have enough dancers. Pay some of those other artists to perform if you need to."

"We're already paying $50,000 a piece for the other four performances," she said defeatedly. But then, half a second later, the reality of her financial situation – *their* financial situation – registered in her vibrant green eyes. She snickered at her brief mental lapse. "What am I saying? We can afford it."

"There you go," Diego said. "The world is ours. There's virtually nothing we can't buy. You're a CEO now. A proprietress. A multimillionaire. We can blow a cool million tomorrow if that's what it takes. You're investing in your brand. Spend whatever you want to spend. Unwind with your family and friends in the VIP sections and throw a hundred grand at some strippers. Tomorrow night is your night. Own it."

Tesla's tongue came out like it always did when she got excited. She set her drink down on the table and climbed onto Diego's lap. His hands glided up her meaty thighs and around to her ass, where they halted for a squeeze, a caress, a sharp slap. Although they'd wiped out on a Jet Ski less than an hour ago, sweet vestiges of her Chanel perfume remained. She lowered her mouth to his and they shared a long, passionate kiss. When their mouths separated her nipples and his dick were equally rigid. He was tempted to roll over on top of her and fuck her right there on the lounge chair.

"How much money have you made since you got all those bricks into the country?" Tesla asked.

"Drug money?"

She nodded.

Diego shrugged. "About seventy-five million. Forty here in the States, the rest in the Caribbean. We sent a big load to Puerto Rico. dumped it on a kingpin who runs La Perla, a treacherous neighborhood on the outskirts of San Juan. we got a few tons into Jamaica, a few more into the Dominican Republic, and we almost got twenty-two hundred kilos into Cuba. damn submarine malfunctioned, though. Engine exploded. The whole thing sank to the bottom of the Caribbean sea."

"People died."

"Of course people died. All four men went down with the sub. I had twenty grand sent to each of their wives. That may not seem like a lot to you, but it's a lot to their families. Enough to hold them over for a few years. Shit, I lost thirty million dollars if you include the cost of the sub."

Tesla stared down at Diego, biting the corner of her succulent bottom lip and regarding him with a dreamy smile. She was clearly fascinated by his wealth, which, considering her tough upbringing, was completely understandable. She'd grown up in abject poverty, in a blighted West Atlanta neighborhood, and now here she was on a two-hundred-million-dollar superyacht, listening to her fiancé complain about a thirty-million-dollar loss and boast about a seventy-five-million-dollar gain. Hardly anyone was impervious to this kind of talk.

"You are such a fucking boss," she said. "What are you going to do with all that cash? I couldn't spend that much money if I tried."

"It's easy to spend, and real estate is one of the best ways to launder it. That house in Malibu is worth forty-nine million alone."

"Don't you have enough money already? Why are you still hustling? I would've stopped and retired a long time ago."

"There's no such thing as enough money. Look at the CEOs of Walmart, Texaco, Nike. they're practically swimming in money. Like Uncle Scrooge in that old duck cartoon. We should be just as fortunate. I want an NFL team, an NBA team. I want the kind of money my father has. Twice what he has. You know …?" He trailed off, reluctant to go on. If he went on. Tesla would know his father's deepest secret. She would know where Alvaro had gotten the cash to finance the start of his own oil-drilling company, and to create the Barranquilla cartel.

"I know what?" Tesla pressed. "That you haven't even told your parents about our engagement?"

Diego was shaking his head and preparing to reveal the fifteen-billion-dollar secret when, in the sky over Tesla's right shoulder, he spotted the helicopter. It was a black 1990 Sikorsky S-76B, one of four in Alvaro's helicopter collections, and it was descending toward the helipad on Snowfall's top deck. Tesla turned and looked up at it, stared for a long moment as the rotor grew louder and closer, then turned back to Diego with a questioning look on her face.

"Well," Diego said, "he may not know about our engagement just yet, but he's about to find out."

Tesla became nervous. Apprehensive. She had mentally prepared herself for this exact moment months in advance, but now as she and Diego walked to the white memory-foam sofas situated in a U shape around the large square coffee table several feet away from the pool, she could think of nothing. Absolutely nothing. The helicopter was on the helipad, Alvaro Santos was making his way down to the main deck, and Tesla Harrison had nothing to say to him.

She felt inferior, as small as a midget in a room full of NBA players. She was seconds away from meeting one of the wealthiest men on the planet, a man with an net worth of $19.2 billion. A man who would soon be her father-in-law.

The boss of a Colombian drug cartel.

"I'll do all the talking," Diego said, as if he could sense her anxiety. "You just sit there and look pretty." He kissed her on the cheek, smacked her on the right buttock, and they sat down next to each other.

"I always look pretty," Tesla muttered. She hated being told what to do. Diego leaned in for a smooch, and she shoved his face away, eliciting a deep guttural chuckle from her husband-to-be.

Ten seconds later, a tall pot-bellied man who bore a striking resemblance to Lazaro walked out onto the main deck. He donned a dark blue suit with no tie and a red pocket square. He had a rolled-up magazine clutched in one fat fist, a thick cigar protruding from his mouth.

He wasn't Alvaro Santos; two days after Diego had placed the gigantic rock on her finger, Tesla had taken Juicy and Rhonda on a week-long getaway to Cancun, Mexico, and they'd spent a lot of time discussing wedding plans and investigating the Santos family online. Tesla had seen a few dozen photos of Alvaro. The hulking man walking toward her now was not him.

"Uncle Mateo!" Diego looked at Tesla. "Babe, this is my uncle, my dad's brother." He stood and gave his uncle a vigorous hug. "Thought you were Al."

"You two need to get dressed. Alvaro wants to see you," Mateo said. The magazine unrolled as he slammed it down on the glass-topped table. Tesla saw that, on the front cover, in the top right-hand corner, there was an inset photo of her face next to Diego's. The caption read, *Santos oil heir engaged to Atlanta stripper!* It was a copy of People magazine, dated April 18, 2005. Today was the fourteenth of April, so the magazine had to be fresh off the press. Mateo pointed at the inset photo. "He's not happy about this." he opened the magazine to a pre folded page that turned out to be a full page photo of Diego putting the ring on Tesla's finger. "Or this. He shouldn't have had to find out about it in a magazine."

Tesla reached for the magazine and flipped through to the end of the article. It was five pages long, and there was one other photo of the ring, a close-up. The article was all about Diego's love life, with photos of several of his exes on a timeline.

Thinking back to the Cancun getaway, Tesla vaguely remembered hearing Rhonda mention something about selling the proposal photos to the highest bidder. They had been in the back of a limo, taking a two-hour ride south from Cancun to visit the Tulum ruins and snorkel in one of the hundreds of cenotes, the natural sinkholes in the limestone. Tesla hadn't taken Rhonda seriously at the time; the three of them had been drinking and laughing and fawning over the engagement ring, and a lot of foolish things had been said.

As they headed inside, Tesla overheard Mateo telling Diego that Alvaro was fuming mad at his lavish three-story penthouse at New Granada Condominiums, the 60-story property he owned in Miami. Mateo spoke to Diego in Spanish, and Tesla was a few feet ahead of them as they headed for the palatial master suite, but she understood every word. Her maternal grandparents, Ronaldo and Lidia Chavez, were both Spanish-speaking Cubans. They lived in Douglasville, Georgia, and sometimes they traveled to Atlanta to visit Claudia and the family. Tesla didn't know them well enough to have learned to speak Spanish fluently, but she understood the language, and she could speak it in short bursts. She ascertained from Mateo's rapid-fire Spanish that Alvaro was furious about the engagement, and that he wanted them to ride the helicopter to the helipad on top of New Granada Condominiums. Posthaste.

The master suite had everything anyone needed, including a walk-in closet, paired bathrooms, and a bedroom that provided private panoramic water views. Guests also had access to a private deck just in front, where Tesla and Diego had spent an hour this morning, debating whose wedding venue idea was the better choice, sipping hot cappuccinos, and watching the sun ease up onto the horizon. Afterward they'd reconnected with their guests in the glassed-in gym for an hour-long workout session.

Tesla took a quick shower, freshened up, and put on a skintight, shoulder less pink Tracy Reese bandage dress over black five-inch Jimmy Choo heels. When she came out of the bathroom, Diego was sitting on the side of the California king bed in a debonair powder blue Zegna suit and shiny dress shoes, strapping a Louis Moinet watch to his wrist. Mateo was nowhere to be seen.

"Uncle Mateo's out walking to Laz," Diego said without looking up.

"Is Laz his son?"

"Yeah, his oldest. Uncle Mateo has three kids. Two boys and a girl, just like my dad. Lazaro, Paco, and Ximena. They're more loyal to me than my siblings could ever be." He looked up to Tesla, and suddenly his lackadaisical expression became awestruck. His eyes crawled upward from her heels to the hem of her dress, which ended two inches below the knee, and continued on up to her hips, her waistline, her perky breasts, and finally to her lips, where they lingered a moment before flitting upward and locking on to hers. "You … are … a goddess," he said voraciously.

Tesla blushed at the compliment. She rolled her eyes and fluttered her lashes.

"I'm so serious," Diego persisted. He got up, walked over to her, and placed his hands on her bare shoulders. "You're the most beautiful woman I've ever laid eyes on. By far. No one else even comes close. I really mean that. Waking up next to you every morning brings me so much joy, so much immeasurable happiness. And then to see you looking like this every day, so flawless even without makeup, showing off that perfect smile. You're incredible. I'm the luckiest man alive."

Tesla could almost feel her heart heating up behind her ribcage. Diego was the only man who'd ever made her feel so good inside. It was as if he'd cast some nefarious spell on her that had completely conquered her love. She slipped her arms around his waist and inhaled his luxurious cologne.

"You don't look too bad yourself," she said.

"You know, I bought that engagement ring the day after we met. It's the most expensive ring Harry Winston has ever designed. I knew I wanted you to be my wife the moment I met you. I 'm sure a lot of guys have told you that before, but I really mean it. Your looks alone were enough. Then I got to know you. I saw how loyal you were to your friends. I saw how much you loved your family, your daughter. And it's all genuine. You carry yourself like a woman. It was your beauty that caught me and your demeanor that kept me."

"Don't get me to cryin'." Tesla said, wiping her eyes before the tears could fall.

"I love you, Tesla. With all my heart."

"I love you too."

He cupped her face in his hands and kissed her on the mouth several times in a row. Then his hands went to her ass for the usual rub, squeeze, and slap. "Ready to go and meet the boss?" He asked.

"About as ready as I'll ever be," Tesla replied. But that could not have been further from the truth. She was not ready to meet her future father-in-law. She was not ready to meet the boss. She could feel the anxiety in the pit of her stomach, weighing her down like a fifty-pound ball of steel. "Hope he likes me."

"He will – eventually. He's not as mean as you'd think. Don Pablo had a presidential candidate assassinated, he had DAS Headquarters bombed, and he even had Flight 203 blown right out of the sky. My dad's role in the coke business is a lot less brutal. He may have been a killer way back in the seventies and eighties, but times have changed. Murder ain't as easy to get away with, you know. He's in his sixties, for heaven's sake. He's a legitimate oil tycoon, a real estate mogul, yet at the same time he's an enemy of the federal government. They want his head for that New York Times journalist's death, and for his ties to the Medellin Cartel back then, he has no choice but to move like a nun. Trust me, you have nothing to fear."

"I'm not afraid of anybody," Tesla said strongly. "I haven't been scared since the day I watched my daddy get his brains blown out right in front of me. I'm just a little nervous, that's all." She peeled away from him and sauntered across the room to the bureau, where she began putting on an impressive array of diamond jewelry. Lugano earrings, a Tiffany tennis bracelet, a Tiffany necklace with 119 two-carat VVS white diamonds, and a new Cartier wristwatch that seemed to be made completely of sparkling baguettes. "I forgot to thank you for this watch, baby."

"You can thank me later," Diego said in a discernibly suggestive tone of voice. "Let's get going. The Sikorsky awaits."

"Give me ten minutes. I need to put my face on. Can't meet your dad looking like this. I'll meet you on the main deck.

Ten minutes stretched into thirty.

Diego stood out on the private deck with Mateo and Lazaro, listening to the two of them discuss the coke shipment Diego planned to run through the Tijuana drug tunnel this evening, and the trucker who'd been pulled over for allegedly speeding on a Wichita highway and busted with six hundred kilos of their product. The trucker, 51-year-old Trevor Redford, was just one of seventeen long-haulers on the Barranquilla Cartel's payroll, though all of them were being made to believe they were working for Mexican drug cartels. His wife and four children had been gunned down inside their Santa Barbara home shortly after his arrest, the fateful result of Trevor's seven-point-two-million-dollar mistake of driving too fast on a Kansas interstate.

While Laz and Mateo talked, Diego perused the People magazine article. He couldn't suppress the thoughtful grin that formed as he looked at a two-year-old photo of his ex Heather Modine that had been snapped at the 2003 AVN Awards, when she'd won Best Anal Scene and Blowjob of the year. She was holding up her two awards on the red carpet, draped in a flowing yellow gown that was sheer with shimmering sequins. Her resemblance to Tesla was startling. She was Dominican and Puerto Rican, with a long mane of hair, a fat round ass, and the same skin complexion Tesla possessed. Her eyes were a lambent brown, her lips weren't as full, and her boobs had been surgically enhanced, but the resemblance was there.

The photo of Camila and Diego walking hand-in-hand had been taken as they were leaving a popular West Hollywood restaurant on the eve of Camila's nineteenth birthday. She had on a backless white Louis Vuitton catsuit over strappy mules. At the time Diego had been the hottest new male model in the fashion industry. He still remembered the cute way Camila had shied away from the cameras as the blinding flashes began. He'd put himself between her and the paparazzi until she was seated comfortably inside the Range Rover he'd borrowed from Sofia that weekend. He was reminiscing about the rest of that glorious night when something Uncle Mateo said caught his attention.

"We need you to be Diego's extra set of eyes and ears. Word is, the Mexican cartels are aware of our presence here in the States, and they're not smiling about it. Take extra security measures."

"There's enough cash to go around," Diego said, rerolling the magazine into a tube. He folded his arms defensively. "We're forgiving our own path."

"Right over theirs," Mateo argued. "You see, in their eyes, Colombians only have one role in this business, and that's to produce. Mexicans are supposed to distribute. American gringos are supposed to sell the product to users and bring the cash back to the Mexicans, who in turn spend it with us, the Colombians. A circle of life, you know. Diego, what you're doing is cutting out the man in the middle. You're cutting out the Mexican. Nobody's done that since the days of Don Pable."

"Yeah?" Emboldened by the comparison to his notorious godfather, Diego took a step toward Uncle Mateo. "Well, these are the days of Don Diego. Who needs the Mexican?"

"You need them. We need them. Keep this up and they're going to start dealing exclusively with the Cali and Medellin cartels. We'll lose tens of millions. Might even start a war."

Diego shook his head in dissent. "They'd be idiots to start a war with one of Colombia's biggest cocaine producers. It'd be counterproductive. They need us; we don't need them."

"That's where you're wrong, Diego. The Mexicans are the risk-takers. We're relatively safe. We're not dodging bullets and federal drug busts. We've got foreign dignitaries in our pockets, Colombian politicians and senior military officials, police chiefs and international investment bankers. We're made men, kings on our own chess boards. Let the pawns move ahead of you. Step out in front of them and sooner or later you'll be in checkmate, with no rematches."

Wise words from a cartel veteran.

Never one to disregard sage advice, Diego took a moment to ponder and internalize everything Uncle Mateo had just said. The strategic dialogue would have continued if Rhonda and Tesla hadn't walked out onto the private deck at that very moment. Tesla hooked a thumb in Rhonda's direction and said, "The heifer sold the engagement photos for almost two hundred thousand dollars."

"I told her about this weeks ago," Rhonda explained as she toweled herself dry.

Diego shrugged his shoulders dismissively. "News would've gotten out one way or the other. At least it was our best friend who profited from it. Let's hurry up and get going before my old man gets too drunk to rationalize."

Chapter 11

The tension was palpable.

Enzo and his entourage of MOB Piru Bloods were mobbing three cars deep through Zone 6. Bo Jangles led the way in his new red Buick Park Avenue on 24's, followed by their longtime friend Crunk J in his blood-red 1973 Chevy Impala on 24's, and Enzo took up the rear in his spotless red 2005 G-Wagon on 24's of the same color. The back seats of each vehicle were occupied by two wild young Bankhead niggas with guns on their hips and ice in their hearts. The two in Enzo's back seats, Brick boy and Fonzi, were also rappers who'd been in and out of the studio with Enzo all this month, finishing up Enzo's latest mixtape and working on their own projects. Brick boy had an AR-15 assault rifle lying across his lap, a cup of Lean in his hand. Fonzi had two .40-caliber Glocks in the waistband of his Coogi sweatpants, and he too was sipping on some sizzurp.

"I'm telling you, Zo, something rubs me wrong about this nigga," Debbie said. She was driving. The G-Wagon was in her name, though Enzo had made the $15,000 down payment. She glanced over at him as they drove down Glenwood. "I think y'all need to cut him off. Business is business, I understand that, but he's too sheisty to be treated as a friend."

"She ain't wrong on that shit, big bruh," Fonzi said. "He the only one who knew about you frontin' me that half a brick. He dropped me off at my bitch crib right after you

146

gave me the shit, and her door got kicked in not even thirty minutes later. My bitch didn't know I had the shit, so it couldn't have been her."

Enzo ashed his cigarette and nodded his head, saying nothing. He was pretty much feeling the same way about Kilo. Especially since Debbie had pointed out that Kilowas in possession of a gift card that looked a lot like the one she'd had in her purse the night they were robbed and carjacked. Enzo had a lot of love for Kilo, but he was no fool. Something shady was afoot. If not for all the bricks of coke Enzo had stashed at his aunt's house and the $500,000 he owed the plug, he almost certainly would have given the green light for his Bankhead goons to blow Kilo's conniving brains out of his head.

But he couldn't do that. Kilo was spending too much money with him. Way too much. Just two days ago he'd come to Enzo with $97,500 for five bricks, and now he wanted four more. He had Zone 3 on lock, with four different trap houses booming all at once, and he was selling weight to a few other dope boys. Which explained why he was ready to re-up so soon.

Enzo was also selling weight to other dope boys, the biggest of whom was Big Woomp, a long time weight-pusher in Greenville, South Carolina. Woomp had already bought fifteen birds from Enzo. he sent Helen, a bad white bitch he'd been fucking with for years, to cop five bricks from Enzo every Friday. Then there was Lil Dizzy, who was originally from Bankhead but lived in Richmond, Virginia. He'd gotten three bricks from Enzo, and he'd only paid for two so far. Enzo had taken five and a half ounces out of every brick and put in an equal amount of cut. He had two crack houses that were doing numbers. He'd put on four cousins, an uncle, and several fellow gang members. He was back in play, back on top where he belonged.

And it was all because of Tesla.

Puffing on his cigarette, Enzo listened to the radio while Debbie drove. They were listening to a disc jockey on 107.9 FM talk about Gucci Mane and Young Jeezy's beef. A lot of people were taking Jeezy's side because of Big Meech. Word on the streets was that Jeezy had a sizable bounty on Gucci's head. Last week, as Debbie had been dancing at Blazin' Saddles, some guy named Pookie Loc had offered her five grand to set up Gucci Mane. She'd turned down the offer, but other strippers were considering it.

When the disc jockey switched topics and began speaking about a bank robbery that went down at a Chase bank in Athens, Enzo shut off the radio and said, "All I'm focused on right now is gettin' money. That's it. Money, money, money, money. If Kilo really did set me up, it'll come to light. Fonzi, if he set you up, you know what he got comin'. He gon' get it in the end. When I tell y'all to go get the nigga, go get him. Till then let's get money."

"I'm with that, blood," said Brickboy.

Debbie sucked her teeth. "I don't know what's up with y'all A-Town niggas, but I'm from H-Town. The Fifth Ward, to be exact. They call my hood the Bloody Nickel, and do you know why?" She left no room for input. "It's because grimy niggas like Kilo get dealt with. Broad day, late night, inside, outside. Don't matter."

"Now you a gangsta," Enzo said with a drab chuckle.

"Been one," Debbie retorted.

She pulled into the Checkers restaurant parking lot where Kilo's brand-new BMW sedan was parked, cruised into the vacant space beside it, and put the gear in park. Kilo was sitting in the clean white beamer with one of his Zone 3 cronies.

Debbie said, "I'm going in to get me something to eat. Baby, you want anything?"

Enzo told her what he wanted: two spicy chicken sandwiches, extra-large fries with two cups of cheese dip, a large sprite. He would've preferred her hitting the drive-thru, but he knew she didn't want to be around Kilo, so he didn't say a words as she shouldered her purse and hopped out of his truck, clad in a simple t-shirt, jeans, and Nike running shoes, her head wrapped in a Gucci scarf, gold jewelry twinkling on her neck, wrist, and fingers. He watched her fat butt cheeks rise and fall as she crossed the parking lot. There were perhaps a dozen othe hood niggas and bitches in the parking lot, and every one of them stopped what they were doing to watch her walk. Catcalls ensued with every comment being about Debbie's meaty derriere.

"Man, blood," Brickboy said, "You *always* got the baddest bitches. Tesla, Stacy, Marquita, and now this bad lil bitch. Shit. you either got a helluva mouthpiece or you got the best luck in the world."

"All you gotta do is getcha money up. That's all you gotta do. Pull up in something like this. Stack a hundred thousand and spend it all with the plug. Turn that shit into two or three million. You'll be fucking actresses." He buzzed his window down and flicked his cigarette out just as Kilo stepped out of the Beamer and approached his door.

"Piru love," Kilo said, reaching in to shake Enzo's hand.

Reluctantly, Enzo did the MOB Piru handshake with Kilo. then Kilo handed him a brown leather MCM backpack. Enzo unzipped it and found it full of rubber-banded stacks of cash. He passed it behind him and told Fonzi to count it. He listened to Kilo complain about Juicy, who'd abruptly broken up with him and put him out of her house early last month.

"It's all good, though. She lost a million-dollar nigga. Bitch cut me off to go chasing behind them rich Colombians. Like they gon' cut her in on some shit. Funky bitch." He adjusted an icy watch on his right wrist. "I just dropped eighty on this watch, blood. On Piru. when I pull up to Tesla's tomorrow night, I'm throwing ten bands just for the fuck of it."

Enzo believed him. Everything about Kilo screamed money, from the sparkling diamonds on his neck and wrists to the snow-white BMW parked behind him. He even smelled like money. A part of Enzo's brain wondered where and how Kilo had acquired so much money in such a short amount of time; another, wiser part knew. Kilo was a grimy motherfucker. He'd probably used the $14,000 Enzo gave him the night of their carjackings to pay for the diamonds in his watch. Enzo didn't want to think about it; the mere thought of doing business with someone who might have played a part in the robbery was too much to bear. It was a struggle to keep himself from confronting Kilo.

The gods were on Enzo's side. His phone rang at that very moment. It was Stacy, his daughter Jasmine's mother. At the same moment, some gold-digging hood chick yelled for Kilo, and when Kilo saw that she was unequivocally the most attractive girl in her crew, he waved her over and leaned back against the driver's door of his car to seal the deal.

Stacy had news, big news, but she wasn't giving it up for free. "I'ma need some money for this," she said, her voice replete with excitement. "It's about your car. The one they took."

"What about it?"

"Can I get some money or what? I need a few thousand to get me a new truck."

"Bitch, if you don't tell me what the fuck –"

"Okay, wait. Shit. Chill out. This dike chick I know from Edgewood just slipped up and told me something."

"Told you what?" Enzo was looking back at Fonzi and Brickboy as they counted the cash. He saw that every bill – mostly fifties and hundreds – was bank-new, which unnerved him a little. Drug money was usually dirty money.

"Okay, listen," Stacy said. "So this dike chick I work with had been coming at me strong ever since I started working, but she kept pressing me and pressing me until I finally gave up and let her give me some head on our lunch break the other day. Oooh, and let me tell you –"

"Get to the point."

"Okay, okay," Stacy said, tittering. "So we went on break today, right, and she told me she had something for me. On the walk to her car, she started telling me about this Chanel bag she had been holding on to for a while. I asked where she got it from, and she said, 'I got it from the girl that's on all the fliers for that new strip club on Piedmont. We robbed that ho about a month ago.' I tried to get her to tell me more but she wouldn't talk about it. She did give me the purse, though. It got your girl's social security card in it and everything. Debra Leiane Hicks, right?"

Enzo clenched his teeth. "What's her name?"

"Sierra Nichols. I can find out where she lives, but your girl should be able to find that out for you. Sierra's brother Shawn is one of them down-low gay niggas. He be getting his dick sucked all the time by gay-ass Quincy Clark, your girl Debbie's cousin."